Invitation to Danger

INVITATION
TO
DANGER

Pat Phillips

Thorndike Press • Chivers Press
Thorndike, Maine USA   Bath, England

This Large Print edition is published by Thorndike Press, USA and by Chivers Press, England.

Published in 2000 in the U.S. by arrangement with Maureen Moran Agency.

Published in 2000 in the U.K. by arrangement with the author.

U.S. Hardcover 0-7862-2592-0   (Candlelight Series Edition)
U.K. Hardcover 0-7540-4195-6   (Chivers Large Print)
U.K. Softcover 0-7540-4196-4   (Camden Large Print)

The text of this Large Print edition is unabridged.
Other aspects of the book may vary from the original edition.

Set in 16 pt. Plantin by Rick Gundberg.

Printed in the United States on permanent paper.

British Library Cataloguing in Publication Data available

Library of Congress Cataloging-in-Publication Data

Phillips, Pat.
    Invitation to danger / Pat Phillips.
        p. cm.
    ISBN 0-7862-2592-0 (lg. print : hc : alk. paper)
    1. Actors — Fiction. 2. Large type books. I. Title.
PS3566.H498 I58 2000
    813'.54—dc21
                                                    00-023443

Invitation to Danger

Chapter 1

Wind-whipped leaves skittered along the
sidewalk as Julie Brown carried her groceries
home. Seeing the store thronged with shop-
pers buying food for Thanksgiving had made
her sad. She thumped open the screen door
to her apartment, fumbling in her pocket for
the key. It was childish to feel this way. She
was independent at last, a state she had
craved during the childhood years spent at
home, but being alone at Thanksgiving was
more than she had expected.

The apartment seemed unnaturally silent
without her roommate's blaring record player.
Though she had often pleaded with her to
turn the thing off, today she would welcome
the earsplitting din of Dottie's favorite rock
group, if only to destroy the tomblike silence
of the empty rooms. Not that Dottie had not
invited her to go home to Nebraska with her.
But Julie had refused, making the excuse that
her mother might call with a last-minute invitation. Dottie might have been convinced by

the lie, but Julie was not, for lie is what it was, an event as improbable as snow in July.

After switching on the light, Julie unpacked the groceries on the battered kitchen table. The decor was Early Depression, complete with stained wallpaper in a fading assortment of flowers and fruit. The design contrasted hideously with their latest auction find, a wooden table and chairs painted fluorescent purple.

Julie wondered if Dottie was having the fun she had expected to have. A handsome male relative, who had been Dottie's ideal for years, was to join them at the Kolb farm for Thanksgiving. This November Dottie was convinced that she would make him sit up and take notice. Lots of luck, Julie murmured to herself as she reluctantly forced herself into action.

The groceries put away, she toasted a cheese sandwich. With the radio playing and the smell of food appetizing, the kitchen seemed almost normal. Dottie would be furious if she knew Julie intended to stay here for the holiday. Brimming with contagious good spirits, Dottie could not bear to think of anyone being lonely or sad, which was why Julie had made up the lie. To tell her friend that her stepfather had forbidden her entry to her home, just like in melodramas of old, would have pierced Dottie's warm heart with maternal love and protection. Driven from home! That was the expression. To think about it brought a bitter smile to Julie's soft mouth. She still could not understand her stepfather's reasoning behind the banishment. He gladly paid her college tuition, boasting to friends about her achievements, yet he did not want her to come home. It was almost as if he felt unable to share even a part of her mother's affection. Life between them had been stormy from the start, the final disappointment coming when her mother had relayed his message, asking her not to come home for Thanksgiving. "Shall we try for Christmas, darling?" Mother had plaintively added in her postscript.

Brooding, her head propped on her hand, Julie fingered her heavy chestnut hair, mentally reviewing past arguments. Pete had not been the right husband for Mom, and she had said so; he drank too much, he was a bully, and his job took him away from home too often. After Dad's death, following a long battle with cancer, Mom needed to be cosseted. Pete Jordan seemed the most unlikely choice for that task her mother could have chosen, but choose him she did, and Julie knew it was time she grew up and accepted the unpleasant fact. At least some good had come from the marriage. Realizing the golden opportunity to remove the thorn from his side, Pete had offered Julie a paid-for college tuition in another town, any town, so long as it was not St. Joseph. Understanding the strings attached, Julie had nevertheless accepted his offer. She had been unable to attend college after high school because Dad's medical expenses had taken all their savings, so she had worked at a boring office job for three depressing years, helping her mother battle through the emotional drain of terminal illness. Now, four years older than the others in her class, she felt a misfit. By chance she had stumbled on Dottie Kolb, who was another old-age pensioner, Dottie having missed schooling due to illness, and uniting last May, the girls had rented this shabby duplex across the street from the campus and become independent.

A movement at the front door made her start. In this shotgun-style house, the three rooms forming their apartment opened into each other, giving a clear view to the front door from the kitchen. A male figure in a bulky overcoat blocked the glass storm door, and uneasily Julie remembered that she had only latched the screen, leaving the outside door open. The man knocked.

"Hi. Can I help you?" she called cheerfully as she crossed the dingy green carpet to the door, straightening her brown sweater and slacks as she went.

It was gloomy outside and the street lights were on. She and Dottie made a practice of not opening the door after dark, a recent spate of brutal campus attacks prompting this rule. Looking past her own reflection in the glass, Julie recognized the man, and her heart lurched with excitement. Tybalt Shaw was his name, and he lived in the new apartments down the street. He was the drama professor's nephew and the romantic ideal of most of the girls taking the course.

"Sorry to bother you. I think I've got some mail of yours," he explained, flashing a disarming smile.

She unlatched the screen and he came inside. She was surprised to discover that Tybalt was not as tall as she had thought him to be. This was the closest she had ever been to him, though like the others, she had often admired him from afar.

"Thanks. I wonder how they made the mistake," she mumbled woodenly, accepting the two envelopes he held in leather-gloved fingers.

"I guess because you're One Hundred and Twelve A. That's my address, but at the apartment building. Probably an auxiliary mailman filling in for the holiday." He smiled

11

as he spoke, his even white teeth reminding her of a toothpaste commercial.

"Well, thanks again." Julie could have kicked herself. Here was Tybalt Shaw in her apartment, and all she could do was mumble polite foolishness. "Aren't you going home?" she blurted with supreme effort. Surely someone as sought-after as Tybalt wasn't marooned on the half-deserted campus, too.

He nodded, his gray eyes taking on a glassy, metallic gleam as they caught the light. "Oh, sure. As a matter of fact, I'm already a day late. But it's not really home. Just to my grandfather's," he explained, turning to go.

There was a long pause during which Julie thought of a dozen witty things to say and mouthed none of them. She was too conscious of her lack of needed make-up to hide her freckles, of her hair sprouting untidily from its mooring — and of Tybalt smiling at her. He was so beautiful, emitting shock waves of that animal magnetism about which Dottie raved. His light brown hair was thick and wavy, expertly barbered at an exclusive men's hairdresser's in the neighboring town. From the campus grapevine she knew he liked fast cars and girls of the same disposition, and that his grandfather, who was a former Shakespearean actor, was loaded and a little crazy. Her informant had added the latter with a grin, implying that Tybalt must have inherited that trait from him. But Julie didn't find Tybalt Shaw crazy. His heavy-lidded eyes were on her face, and the blood rushed to her fair cheeks at his lazy smile.

"Don't I know you from class?" he asked slowly, his generous mouth curved in what Dottie called his lady-killer grin.

"Well, yes, I guess you've seen me there."

Tybalt glanced at the letters in her hand. "Julie Brown. Of course. I didn't attach you to that name."

He was lying, because she knew he had not bothered to find out who she was before today; she knew, but she did not care. Loneliness and longing for companionship made her bold. "It's really Juliet, but that was too fanciful for me. I've been Julie since grade school."

"Hey, that's interesting. We're a real Shakespearean pair — Tybalt being a bit fanciful for anyone. But what the heck, if I can live with it, so can everyone else."

Desperately searching for something to add so that Tybalt wouldn't know how hard her heart was thumping, Julie offered: "If you don't have to rush off, I've got some coffee made. Would you like some?"

He hesitated, his hand on the door. "Okay. I've got a few minutes."

Julie was conscious of his eyes boring into her back as they walked to the kitchen. Checking her appearance in the steamy mirror over the divan, she saw that the surprise encounter had given her added color. The excitement of his visit had whipped rose to her cheeks, sparkling her green eyes, turning her mouth smiling. Unfortunately the same could not be said for her chestnut hair, which she had wound into an unartistic lump to fit inside her knitted cap for the walk to the store.

While Tybalt took off his impeccably tailored camel overcoat, Julie snatched out the pins so that her thick hair fell in ropes down her back. When he looked up, he was clearly surprised and, from the look on his face, Julie discovered with shocking excitement, interested. What would Dottie say when she told her that Tybalt Heartthrob of Smith College had actually noticed her?

"That's a real improvement. Your hair, I mean. Juliet suits you better than Julie now," he complimented, his gaze sweeping rapidly over her sweater and slacks.

Used to the appraisal, and not finding Tybalt's gaze offensive, Julie thanked him. At least there was nothing wrong with her figure. Small-waisted and slim-hipped, she always felt her shape made up for the lack of classic beauty about her face. It must have been a compensation from her fairy godmother.

"I was blind not noticing you before now —
I mean, introducing myself," Tybalt hastily
corrected. He knew he was caught, but his
bounding self-assurance carried him through.
"Aren't you going home?"

"Not this time."

Tybalt's expression changed as he detected
something unspoken in her hasty dismissal of
the subject. It was as if he had probed her sub-
conscious, and in embarrassment Julie turned
away.

"At least you're one up on me. I haven't any
parents to go home to," he said easily, fingering the handle of his cup.

Julie stared at his elegant hands, slim and
strong and brown. Howard, her sometime
boy friend from English Lit, had hairy, stubby
fingers; he had no charm or class —

"Would you consider something really
wild?" Tybalt was saying in his low, resonant
voice as he leaned across the table, his face
alight with an idea.

"Wild," Julie faltered, coming down to earth
with a thud. What exactly would Tybalt
Shaw's idea of wild be? Was he about to sug-
gest a campus live-in arrangement, with all
conjugal rights?

"Sure, wild, zany. I like you, and I think
Gerald will, too. There's something fragile

about small women, like a medieval painting. You'll be perfect."

Julie began to wonder if Tybalt were sober. His conversation did not make sense. "I'm not sure what you mean," she replied stiffly.

Catching her thoughts, Tybalt laughed. "Oh, Lord, no, this is quite respectable. No campus sin, or anything like that. You can call your folks first to make sure it's all right — if you accept, that is."

"Accept what?"

"I want you to come with me to meet my grandfather. This is really a coincidence. He said to bring a Juliet with me. But first I must explain about him." Tybalt grimaced at the idea. "Gerald Brookham is my mother's father. Her name was Juliet, too. He was a Shakespearean actor, totally hung up on the bard. We all have names to match. People call him eccentric. I think he's crazy. But he's a laugh. He throws lavish affairs at his place. And that house is another story, right out of Olde England slap in the heart of the Ozarks. If you're not doing anything, come with me. It'll be a trip to remember."

Any journey taken with Tybalt Shaw would be a trip to be remembered. Normally cautious of near strangers, Julie hesitated, ignoring the joyous voice that rang in her head. He wants to be with you! He admires you! Say yes

16

before he changes his mind!

"Are you sure he wouldn't mind? After all, he doesn't know me."

"Your name's Juliet. That's reason enough," Tybalt said.

He drummed his fingers on the table, and treacherously Julie wondered what it would be like to be caressed by him. To be kissed. To be held.

"Okay, though I think this must be temporary insanity." Her own voice sounded strange, her words giggly and excited, quite unlike the usual, calm Julie Brown approach. Going anywhere with a man like Tybalt would take the utmost sense and control, for if she wasn't careful she could end up in a difficult situation.

At his insistence Julie called home to leave a message for her mother; then she thrust a couple of changes of clothing and the necessary toilet articles into her suitcase. While she turned clumsily through the drawers, her heart raced, blood turning her oval face rosy and hot. She was going away for a weekend with a man; that was certainly the construction her mother would put on this invitation. But Tybalt's grandfather would be there, and, as he suggested, it would be a house party, other guests as well. With determination Julie turned her mother's smiling photograph face-down on the bureau, for the candid blue gaze made her feel guilty.

They sped around curves in Tybalt's primrose sports car, and Julie hunched down in the seat and decided not to watch. He was a good driver, but his reckless personality showed in the way he handled the foreign car. Belatedly she wondered what had happened between Tybalt and his current romance, Sandi Burns. Surely she would have been his natural choice for the invitation to Avon House. Perhaps Sandi had gone home to her family. Julie was not blind enough to consider her attractions stronger than those of the bouncy, raven-haired cheerleader, the darling of the campus. Tybalt often dated members of the college royal family, so to speak; that was an accepted fact of life. The small enrollment added further stature to their positions, for in the milling thousands of a larger college, Tybalt's charm might have been eclipsed. As it was, here he reigned supreme.

"Will Merky be there, too?" Julie asked, unconsciously using the drama professor's nickname, a parody of his given name, Mercutio.

"I expect so. Poor guy can't afford not to go. Grandfather subsidizes his expensive tastes," Tybalt explained with a frown.

"You sound sorry for him."

Tybalt shrugged. "Not really sorry. I don't

like him enough for that. He's Mom's brother, that's all. Guess it's family loyalty."

Julie was surprised at his statement. Though Merky could be a grouch at times, her feelings toward him hinged on the indifferent. He was the type of person who never elicited emotion until he donned a costume and assumed a theatrical role. Then he blossomed with wit or bravery, depending on his fictional character's attributes.

"He's a good actor, though," she felt obliged to add.

"That's one thing he inherited from Gerald, the only thing. Mother had Gerald's good looks and personality. Poor old Merk was stuck with the intangible talents."

Julie smiled. Poor old Merk was the perfect name for Tybalt's uncle. Sallow-faced, light-haired, he reminded her of a rag doll washed pale by the rain. If she had not known he was related to Tybalt, she would never have guessed it. Though he had inherited the family coloring, on Tybalt the pale eyes assumed magnetic appeal, while the light brown hair shone with gold lights. Poor old Merk was only a shadow of the Brookham image.

By the sharply twisting road Julie knew they were climbing higher into the mountains. The altitude blocked her ears until she gulped hastily to clear them. They had not passed another car for more than thirty minutes. In the distance lights twinkled from isolated homes, but the safety of the valley seemed miles away. Dark shapes of towering trees loomed grimly as they turned into a narrow road leading to immense stone pillars that stood at the entrance to the estate. For a moment fear flashed through her. Here she was, miles from nowhere, with a man she did not know. It was night, and no one knew she was here. What if handsome Tybalt was one of the maniacs she read about, in the papers? What if he was the campus attacker of last spring?

"Getting cold feet?"

His question startled her. Flashing him a sheepish grin, she took a deep breath and tried to relax. "How did you guess?"

"You look apprehensive, to say the least. Look, Julie, there's something I want to tell you before we get there."

Sensing discomfort in his voice, Julie nodded, wondering what Tybalt was going to say to add to her unease.

"Gerald acts crazy, flapping around in fancy dress, sounding like someone out of Shakespeare. Just remember the stage was his whole life. People think he's eccentric because he has money. If he was broke they wouldn't be so kind. Some of the other girls I've brought here —"

He paused at Julie's gasp of surprise. She should have known someone as handsome as Tybalt would have brought other girls here for the weekend, yet she had pretended she was the first. To have her dream dashed so completely was a blow.

"Some of the other girls were afraid," Tybalt concluded.

"Why?"

"I'm not sure. The house can be pretty spooky. I guess that, combined with Gerald, was too lethal a dose. Or maybe they didn't find me entertaining enough to bother staying," he added with a grin, rounding a bend in the twisting drive.

Silhouetted in the headlights was a stone-turreted house. Julie caught her breath, but not in delight. Fear chilled her inexplicably as she stared at the dozens of diamond-paned windows that peered like sightless eyes from beneath a crown of twisted chimneys and stone battlements.

"What do you think? It's pretty fantastic. Even Gerald couldn't afford to build it today. Some tycoon fancied himself an English lord. It's pure eighteen-nineties. A fabulous fake."

Julie swallowed, wondering why the sight of the house had chilled her so. Or was it more the acceptance of her true relationship to

Tybalt that had caused the reaction?

"Be honest with me," she said.

"Sure."

"Am I here instead of Sandi Burns?"

Now it was Tybalt's turn to be uncomfortable. "Sorry. I didn't think you'd mind."

"It's not that I mind. I just want to get things straight from the beginning," Julie said frostily, shielding her pricked ego with reserve. "People like to know when they're merely a stopgap."

"Stopgap is the last thing I'd call you," Tybalt said softly.

Julie felt his hand lightly against hers on the leather seat, felt the spark of his touch, and though she wanted to be angry with him, she could not be. A pathetic, lonely part of her cried out to him, wanting to be cherished and admired even if it was only for a long weekend.

"Come on, let's meet the bard. I haven't seen Gerald for nearly a month."

Chapter 2

"Ah, Tybalt, what a pleasure to see you," a resonant voice boomed as Gerald Brookham emerged from the murky recesses of the house, hand extended.

A sour-faced maid had opened the door, admitting them to the chill, paneled interior of a poorly lighted hall. Almost at once Tybalt's grandfather appeared, alerted by the flashing headlights as they came up the driveway.

"Hi. Sorry I'm late," Tybalt apologized easily, gripping the outstretched hand in a firm clasp.

"Quite all right. You're the last to arrive. We've been waiting for you, but I knew you'd come. Man of his word, Tybalt. And this is Juliet."

Julie caught her breath in surprise, wondering how he knew her name when she was not even expected. Gerald Brookham lightly took her fingers, gallantly stooping over her hand to kiss it. His mouth felt chill and dry, like old parchment. As he straightened up she looked directly into his face, and what she saw made her shiver. His piercing eyes were unfathomable beneath heavy-hooded lids; his stern, lined face seemed to be carved from marble, so perfectly chiseled were the contours. Above a high-domed brow his receding hair shone white, a short, pointed beard wagging on his chin emphasizing his speech. To add to the strangeness of his appearance, he was clad in a black voluminous kimono edged with gold braid, looking for all the world like Merlin the Magician. All he needed to complete the picture were a conical hat and some gold moons and stars.

"I didn't know you were expecting me, Mr. Brookham," Julie managed.

"I'm always expecting Juliet," he explained. "She is ever-present."

"This really is Juliet — Juliet Brown," Tybalt introduced her.

Gerald Brookham seemed momentarily puzzled as he gently cupped Julie's chin, turning her face toward the feeble light to study her closer. Though she did not enjoy the gesture, Julie knew he meant no offense, so she smiled and waited for the scrutiny to be over.

"Yes. She is very like your dear mother. Her name was Juliet, too, my dear. Has this lad told you?"

Julie nodded, relieved when he stepped back a pace and indicated a shadowy doorway. "It's very good of you to have me as your guest, Mr. Brookham."

"A pleasure, my dear, a pleasure. Perhaps before this weekend is out we shall perform yet another memorable scene from the immortal bard." With this Gerald Brookham disappeared almost as abruptly as he had come.

Tybalt slipped his arm lightly about Julie's shoulders. "Bananas, but quite a laugh," he hissed.

His humor dispelled some of her dismay. To begin with, Julie had little idea what the man had been talking about. "He's pretty corny. What's all that immortal-bard stuff?"

"Now, don't dismiss it so lightly. At Grandfather's gatherings the guests usually perform a scene from a chosen play. He gets pretty wrapped up in it. I'm supposed to bring a girl from the drama course with me to play a character. Last time they did *Macbeth*. Things didn't turn out too well. I was dating Deanie Jones; remember, the girl who was attacked on campus, then took an overdose of pills?"

"I remember. She wasn't really a friend of mine, but I'd seen her around." How could she forget the incident? The local papers had carried little else that week. The connection, coupled with her own unease, did not add to her security. Could the amateur dramatics have been frightening enough to make someone take her own life?

"What scared her about *Macbeth*?" Julie felt compelled to ask. She shivered in the draughty hall, instinctively stepping closer to Tybalt for warmth and protection.

"Deanie freaked out. She thought the blood on Lady Macbeth's hands was real. It must have been the attack that unbalanced her. She was roughed up pretty bad — here's Gerald again."

Light flooded the hallway, brightening the somber paneling and pinpointing crossed lances and a dented shield above the front door. A worn, red Turkish carpet covered the floor. An enormous knobbly hallstand decorated with Shakespearean scenes dominated the narrow room, reaching out grasping arms loaded with wrought-iron books. It was so hideous, Julie was morbidly fascinated by the scenes of violence and bloodshed superimposed on a bright crimson backing. The sight of the gruesome hallstand and her uneasy reaction to both Gerald and Avon House, compounded now by visions of a demented Deanie Jones, made Julie wish she had never come. Yet there was still the pleasant reassurance of Tybalt's arm on her waist as he ushered her through the doorway to the living room.

The room was lavishly decorated, giving the impression of baronial splendor of centuries past. Though there were wall sconces and a heavy chandelier hanging from the oak beams, the lighting was too dim for comfort, and Julie resisted the urge to glance behind her to the shadowed corners. Heavy, carved oak chairs padded in scarlet velvet stood beside the hearth, where a fire blazed in the huge grate. Above the gray stone mantel was a painting of the young Gerald Brookham as Hamlet, his piercing eyes seeming to follow Julie as she walked across the room.

Merky Brookham stumbled to his feet, openly surprised to see her. Beside him his wife surveyed Julie with a bored air, as if the quantity and quality of Tybalt's girl friends did not interest her.

"Miss Brown! What a surprise," Merky gasped. His shock at seeing her accompanying Tybalt was so obvious, Julie felt embarrassed.

"Juliet, dear, this is Sarah, Mercutio's wife," Gerald boomed, his formerly severe expression softening as he took Julie's hand to present her.

Mrs. Brookham inclined her head, managing a tight smile. There was an Oriental look

27

about her smooth face and slanted eyes, the illusion enhanced by a towering plaited chignon of ebony hair; however, when Merky married her last year, she was disappointingly revealed as plain Sarah Pence, a nurse from Hartford. Perhaps the exotic suggestion of the Orient in her looks added spice to poor Merky's otherwise dull life.

"How do you do? I think I might have seen you on campus," Sarah allowed, uncrossing her ankles as she leaned forward. The movement drew Julie's attention to Sarah's large feet, encased very unglamorously in black orthopedic shoes.

"I'm glad to meet you, Mrs. Brookham. Perhaps you've seen me at one of the plays."

"Now, Juliet, child, we only use first names here," Gerald said. "And please, my dear, don't be tempted to use that ghastly nickname — Merky. It makes my blood boil."

Forewarned by his words, Julie knew she would have to guard her tongue, for she never thought of Professor Brookham as anything but Merky. To please her strange host, however, she would make the effort.

Glasses of port were served, and Julie perched uncomfortably on the edge of her chair, sipping the drink and waiting for the opportunity to go to her room. She was tired. The two-hour journey itself had not been exhausting, it was more her emotional response to all that had happened since the unexpected knock on her door this afternoon. Now all Julie looked forward to was a bath and a comfortable bed. She would even welcome the warmth of her corduroy car coat, which had been whisked away by the silent maid, for this room had such strong drafts that they moved the newspapers on the coffee table. The curtains were a heavy plush velvet and did not stir as the icy currents explored the large room. Gerald Brookham obviously believed in Shakespearean heating as well.

Seeing her shiver, Tybalt pulled off his sweater and offered it to her. "Grandfather isn't much on central heat — he says it dries the skin and ages you," he confided.

Julie was grateful to him. Tybalt was really much quieter away from his natural habitat at Smith. Maybe this was the real man, and that other just a fascinating character he played, rather like his uncle Merky's habit, springing from dissatisfaction with his own personality.

The others made small talk and rehashed the last production at Cave Point, the local theatrical colony that Gerald Brookham funded in thirty wooded acres adjoining his mansion. His generosity was unbounded, his fame known on both sides of the Atlantic, yet Julie did not like him; something beyond his strangeness and flamboyant language prevented it.

After what seemed an eternity, the maid showed her to her room. The hard-faced, middle-aged woman was morose, and though Julie would have liked to question her about the strange old house, she did not have the nerve to attempt to penetrate her forbidding exterior.

"Bathroom's next door. Mr. Brookham rings a gong for breakfast. Be ready by eight." With that the maid marched away, her back ramrod-stiff.

Julie surveyed her dingy room. A lingering odor of gas permeated the air. A feeble gas fire glowed in the large hearth where logs should have burned. The green brocade curtains and matching bedspread added to the air of antiquity; a carved bedstead and dressing table, and a dusty green silk lampshade on the marble-based floor lamp, belonged to the turn of the century. Julie half expected to find corsets and feather fans stored in the heavy wardrobe, but to her dismay it was empty. Wherever Gerald Brookham spent his money, it was certainly not on furnishings.

Fortunately the bedsheets were clean and aired. Julie opened her suitcase on the floor, stooping to remove her night clothes. This room was so depressing, she had already decided to spend as little time in it as possible. Without Tybalt the unfriendly atmosphere of the house was hard to overcome, and she shivered in sudden fright at the creaking of the door. No one was there. The maid had not latched it, and grasping the glass knob, Julie banged the door shut.

In the morning, awakened by the reverberating tones of a Chinese gong, Julie flung on her clothes and bolted downstairs, not wanting to make a bad impression by being late to breakfast.

The meal was almost cold. Wading through a morass of soggy scrambled eggs, Julie glanced about brightly at the other diners. "This is a fascinating house, spooky but interesting," she commented, trying to make conversation. Merky glanced up from his plate and grinned a sickly, sheepish grin before going back to the morning paper.

"You might say that," Tybalt agreed, coming to her rescue. "These old mausoleums don't fascinate me too much."

"Tybalt, you should be ashamed!" Sarah chided with a smile, stopping behind his chair, her hand lingering a moment on his shoulder. Her voice was husky as she added, "You'll probably inherit this magnificent home someday. You must uphold the Brookham tradition."

"What about Merky? Isn't he in line for it, too? Maybe you'll be the one to inherit this *magnificent home* instead," Tybalt snapped, surprising Julie by his abrupt attitude.

Sarah paused, her large hands gripping the back of Tybalt's chair until the knuckles whitened. "Yes," she said at last, "I'm sure I shall enjoy this home someday. I've lived here so long, I think of it as mine already."

Finding her statement strange, Julie looked questioningly at Tybalt as Sarah went to the buffet to pour some coffee, leaving a lingering waft of Forest Flower perfume in her wake.

"*Dear* Aunt Sarah used to be my mother's nurse."

"Oh, I didn't know," Julie blurted, trying to recall the newspaper report of the wedding. Of course she had known Sarah was a nurse, but she hadn't thought of her working here.

"Yes, my dear, for four very long years. So you see why I'm so familiar with this house." Sarah treated her to a vague smile. "I know every nook and cranny like the back of my own hand."

Later, when Sarah and Merky had retired to their own room, and Gerald snoozed noisily beside the hearth, Tybalt came to sit beside Julie on the couch beneath the windows. Suspecting ulterior motives, and hesitant to allow him the opportunity to romance her, Julie moved to the far end of the mushroom silk couch. Talking would maintain respectability until she had figured out this fascinating and somewhat dangerous male. Be sensible and level-headed, she warned herself, taking a deep breath before forming a bright, inquisitive smile.

"Now, Tybalt, you must tell me what's expected of me here. I don't want to let you down," she began.

He blinked, taken aback by her breezy statement. "Oh, not much," he mumbled, edging closer.

"The theatricals you spoke of; I certainly want to acquit myself admirably," Julie bubbled, the words sounding like an essay. What are you doing? she asked herself, appalled by this foolish pretense, yet unable to stop. "I wasn't the star of my high-school drama for nothing. I know a little Shakespeare — that is what he's so fond of, isn't it?"

"Oh, yeah, addicted to it, I would say." Tybalt drew back. His hand had been inches from hers; his long elegant fingers had been curved to hold her own. Now he spun a faded gold tassel on the pillow beside him. "Look, Juliet Brown, let's get something straight. I'm not intending to expose you to a 'fate worse than death,' as the Victorian novelettes would

33

say. Relax. You're so uptight I don't know you."

Chastised, Julie found the blood rushing to her face. "Sorry. I guess you're right. The journey was pretty tiring, and I didn't get much rest last night in that lumpy old bed. Guess it made me crabby."

Tybalt nodded in sympathy. "Next time you can't sleep, look me up — second floor, end of the corridor. Anyway, seriously, the big day isn't until Friday, so you can relax till then. Nothing too great's expected of you. You just dress up and do what you're told. No one expects you to get an Academy Award, you know."

Wondering if he was making fun of her, Julie sneaked a look at him from beneath lowered lashes. He smiled, but the expression was not unkind.

"Is that what Deanie Jones tried to do?" she could not help asking; then at once she was sorry. His face tightened, his eyes going ice-cold.

"Forget Deanie Jones. She was a mixed-up kook. A pretty one, but nevertheless a kook. If you keep dragging it up, I'll be sorry I told you about her. I didn't have to, you know. It's none of your business how many girls I bring here. A whole harem if I want to."

His angry words startled her. He probably

felt responsible for Deanie's suicide, and that made him react so intensely about her.

"Don't get excited. I barely knew the girl and couldn't care less how many times she came here or what went on between you."

"That's better." Tybalt grinned, relaxing once more. "That's the kind of female spirit I recognize. For a moment you had me worried. I thought you were a different breed."

Julie forced a smile. Of all the conceited things! Tybalt was certainly sure of himself. That smug overconfidence must have been generated by the hordes of adoring females who sighed in ecstasy when he passed by.

"Are we going to spend this long weekend taking cuts at each other?" she asked, deciding to speak her mind. All this nonsense about being witty and sparkling, of living up to Tybalt's expectations of an attractive female, was too much of an effort to keep up.

"You disappoint me. I thought you enjoyed it."

"A little goes a long way. It's bad enough being an eleventh-hour replacement without having to be Miss Personality Plus. To be truthful, the house gives me the creeps. And the company isn't much better," Julie added, glancing pointedly toward Gerald Brookham rumbling and whistling beside the hearth.

"An honest female. I can't believe my ears."

"You can cut that out, too. I'm me, not some carbon copy of what every college male wants in his Christmas stocking."

"Okay. You've made your point. I guess I have been pretty trite. Not knowing you, I fell into the old pitfall of typecasting — lonesome single girl, pining for romance — you are pining for romance, aren't you?" Tybalt grinned disarmingly at her.

"At the right time with the right man I may consider it."

"Fine. At least you've left the door open. Now, what do you want to do with yourself today? I give guided tours of the estate, no extra charge."

"Well, this is Thanksgiving Day, though it hardly seems like it. Shouldn't we be watching the parades or the football game or something?" Julie offered lamely.

"I'm too old for Mighty Mouse, and the games haven't started. Any more crackerjack suggestions?"

Bristling with annoyance at his attitude, Julie slowly and deliberately stood up, drawing herself up to her full five feet three inches. "Yes, and it's the best one to date. I'm going to my room until dinner."

Though she would have loved to turn and see his expression, Julie forced herself to keep going. After majestically sailing up the dark stairs and entering her bedroom, her calm reserve disintegrated. Sitting here alone in turn-of-the-century gloom was not her idea of how to spend an exciting Thanksgiving. She had blown it with Tybalt now. It was only nine-thirty, she discovered, looking at her watch in dismay.

"Are you in there, Julie?" There was no mistaking Sarah Brookham's tone of mock concern.

"Yes, come in."

Sarah stood in the doorway, a fixed smile on her face. "Is anything wrong?"

"No. Just wondering what to do with myself, that's all."

Sarah's face relaxed, and she came inside the room. "That can be a problem here, I must admit. Where's Tybalt?"

The way she glanced around the room, it seemed as if she had expected him to be hiding in the closet. "Downstairs, I expect. He's not here, if that's what you're thinking."

"No, I thought nothing of the sort," Sarah hastily corrected. "You mustn't be so much on the defensive. I want us to be friends. After all, we are both weekend guests."

"It's not defensive. I thought maybe you suspected me of hiding him under the bed or something." Julie laughed, trying to lighten the mood. Sarah made her uneasy. It was as if she were under constant surveillance. Even now as she spoke of friendship Sarah's dark eyes evaluated the contents of Julie's open suitcase beside the dressing table.

"Well, the morals of some of those girls at Smith leave much to be desired. I might expect them to hide a whole regiment in their rooms. Nothing personal, of course," Sarah added hastily, realizing her implication.

"Of course."

"You must come downstairs to help me, dear. You can't stay here by yourself. Unless you want to write to someone."

"I'm not much of a letter writer. I usually call instead."

"I see. Then you do want to let your family know you arrived safely?"

Recalling the letter from her mother, hurt stabbed her afresh, making her blurt: "No. There's no one interested in that information."

Sarah smiled. "That's as well. We have no phone. I was going to direct you to the colony."

"No phone!"

"That's right. It is strange, I admit. One of Gerald's eccentricities. He doesn't like modern inventions. Do come downstairs. We're making cornucopias. You look so artistic, I'm sure you'll do them beautifully."

Gulping at the generous compliment, Julie followed Sarah into the chilly hall.

Tybalt was nowhere to be seen. The dining table was heaped with dried leaves and berries and platters of polished fruit. Making cornucopias seemed as good an occupation as any. While they worked, Sarah told Julie about her own struggle to make ends meet while studying nursing and supporting a younger brother. The shared confidences made the time pass quickly, and Julie found herself telling Sarah about her father's illness and death. The confidences stopped there. It was too soon to want to tell her about her mother and Pete Jordan. Mr. and Mrs. Jordan. Even saying the name to herself was distasteful.

The cornucopias finished, they stood back to admire them. On the polished mahogany table the overflowing wicker forms of red and yellow apples, oranges, nuts, fiery leaves, and grasses added the perfect autumn touch.

"Beautiful," Sarah complimented, slipping her arm about Julie's shoulders in friendship. "We eat at twelve-thirty sharp. Gerald insists on it. I know you're probably used to a big turkey dinner with all the trimmings, and I hope you're not disappointed, but we are having baked trout and spinach soufflé. Gerald usually has that on Thursdays. Our true feast will be on Friday, when he has some of the students in from Cave Point Colony. You'll like them, my dear."

"Well, I'm surprised. I guess it'll be the first time I've eaten that for Thanksgiving dinner. But it's okay."

"Good. You're such a nice understanding girl. Why don't you take a walk in the grounds till then? The sun's gone in, but I'm sure it's not too cold," Sarah paused, then winking archly, she added, "As a matter of fact, you might just bump into Tybalt while you're out."

"That's all right. We're not getting along too well at the moment."

"Oh, what nonsense. Tybalt told me how much he thought of you. He's gone over to the theater with a message from Gerald. You'll probably meet him on the way back. The walk over there's so pleasant. Wooded and picturesque."

"Thanks. It sounds like a good idea," Julie said half-heartedly. At least walking in the grounds would get her out of the house, though meeting Tybalt was not what she felt like doing after their morning exchange. Still, if he had told Sarah about his feelings for her, things could be looking up.

"Julie, do you like dogs?" Sarah called.

Pausing in the doorway, Julie grinned. "Love them."

"Well, I don't know if you'll still feel that way after you've met Caesar," Sarah said with a smile. "He's rather a brute. But he means well."

"Is he your dog?"

"No. Gerald's. Although he spends such little time with him, Caesar probably doesn't know it." Sarah laughed at her own humor, and Julie smiled faintly, anxious to leave, the scent of freedom tingling in her veins. "When you've got your coat on, let me know. I'll get him. You might be glad of the company."

Caesar was bigger than Julie had expected. The large black Labrador waited by the door to the garden room, his head resting on his paws. At the sight of her he bounded to his feet, loping down the stone-flagged passage to greet her. Huge paws nearly toppled Julie off balance, and she gasped as she steadied herself against the wall.

"He's very friendly." Sarah came from the shadows as if she had been watching the meeting to see how it went before she revealed her presence.

"It's lucky I'm not afraid of dogs," Julie said sharply, annoyed by Sarah's lack of concern. "This elephant could give someone a heart attack."

"Yes, I see what you mean," Sarah agreed, opening the door for her. "Have a good time.

41

And if he runs away, don't worry. He knows his way back."

Caesar needed no coaxing. As soon as the fresh, cold scent of earth and woodland blew indoors, he bounded over the doorstep, tail waving, and plunged into the shrubbery.

Chapter 3

The wind moaned eerily through the dying leaves of the trees. Tybalt was nowhere to be seen. Julie walked briskly through the woodland hoping to find him soon, for the more she thought about Sarah's assurances that he felt romantically inclined toward her, the more anxious she was to confront him to see if it was fact, or merely Sarah's social chatter. Though loathe to admit it, she hoped Sarah had told the truth.

However many acres this estate comprised, she had not intended to cover them alone, for even here the forlorn aspect of the house penetrated cold fingers. Shivering, she pulled her blue knitted cap around her ears. Her companion suddenly rustled through the undergrowth, startling her by his appearance; she had assumed that Caesar had vanished into the woods long ago.

"Here, boy, good dog," she called.

Wagging his tail, the Labrador bounded to her. There was something long and red trailing from his mouth. For a moment of panic Julie wondered if it was a creature he had killed; then reason told her it was only a rag.

"Come on, give it to me."

Eyes rolling piteously, Caesar groveled on the earth before relinquishing his prize: a bedraggled, half-chewed red scarf. Smiling at his antics, Julie swung the scarf on her arm. She might use it for a lead if Caesar became adventurous. Whether he knew it or not, this big dog was going to accompany her back to the house.

"Hey, Julie!"

She turned in the direction of the voice and saw Tybalt sprinting along the path from the lake. In a minute he was at her side, out of breath but relieved to find her.

"Sarah told me you were by the lake."

"I don't know why, since she told me you went to the theater," Julie said in surprise, wondering what game Sarah Brookham was playing. Had she hoped Julie would be lost in these woods, or was she trying to scare her by sending her out alone into such a lonely area? But why give her the dog as a companion — unless she assumed Caesar would run away?

"Guess she got her wires crossed. Glad you're over your hibernation. Dinnertime's hours off, and it sure would have been lonely — for both of us."

44

Julie smiled at his words. Sarah was right. It appeared as if Tybalt was ready to be friends. "A woman's prerogative: I changed my mind."

"Fine. Been having fun chasing Caesar?"

"There's not much chasing going on, but he makes me feel safer. This place is even creepy outdoors."

They walked to the edge of the clearing and stood on a rise of ground overlooking the lake. The sun came out, though it was still cold on the exposed point, and Julie huddled close to the comforting warmth of Tybalt's side. He smiled down at her and slipped his arm protectively around her shoulders.

"Let's find someplace more sheltered," he suggested.

Julie's sense told her to say no. Tybalt was the last person with whom she should share a secluded spot. He made her arms prickle with goose bumps when he touched her. But today she was deaf to the voice of reason.

"Okay. How about those rocks? It's a cave!"

He hesitated, his face momentarily clouded. Then he shrugged. "Sounds as good as anywhere."

When she would have explored the chill recesses of the cave, Tybalt laughingly pulled her back. The dog scrambled up the craggy exterior and disappeared through the scrub oak, pursuing a wild creature, his nose to the ground.

"That's a great dog. Knows when to make himself scarce."

Julie smiled at Tybalt's words, and she stuffed the old red scarf in her pocket and un-buttoned her coat. This side of the rocks was a sun trap. She closed her eyes, smiling in pleasure at the warmth. Tybalt moved closer until she could feel the whispery touch of his hair prickling her face. Half afraid to open her eyes, she felt his cheek against hers forcing her to look at him, so close she could see the separate dark lashes around his eyes, where the gray iris was flecked with black, and could discern the beginnings of a mustache dusting his upper lip. She studied his mouth, wondering if he would kiss her, or if he would try forcefully to claim her affection. They were alone. Caesar would certainly be no help in the crunch. To her surprise Julie discovered that she wanted Tybalt to make a pass at her, wanted to know he was definitely attracted to her for herself and not as some spur-of-the-moment replacement. Yet she was afraid, too. Why did it have to be Tybalt Shaw, of all people? If the man beside her had been Howard, she would have been in total command of her emotions. Howard was very easy to repel. Probably because he didn't matter very much to her, and Tybalt did.

"Are you still sore because I invited you — instead of Sandi, I mean?"

Julie shut her eyes tight. She could not face those points of boring light that penetrated her brain, too afraid that her own emotion was plainly discernible. She could feel his eyes on her, yet not looking at him was easier. "I should be."

"Why? I'm not going to marry Sandi, or anything."

Not going into the "or anything," Julie asked, "Do you love her?"

"No. Did you think I did?"

"How should I know?" Now she opened her eyes and found him smiling at her, his mouth curved to display his teeth in what she was sure was a completely artful way. He probably practiced in front of the mirror, knowing how attractive the expression made him look.

"You know, you're the only girl I haven't been able to figure out," he whispered, reaching out to take a strand of hair from her brow. His fingers were warm and tantalizing on her skin, and Julie shivered, hating herself for betraying her emotion, for being so weak.

"I didn't know you wanted to bother figuring me out."

"Oh, come on, you're not serious."

Her heart thundered beneath her coat, and she tried to keep her hands from trembling as he leaned over her, imprisoning her with his arm.

"The way I see it, all girls are a challenge to you."

He laughed at her statement. "Is that the current idea circulating through Smith?"

Julie grinned, finding she liked the verbal exchange. It gave her time to put her emotions in order. "You'd be surprised what we say about you."

"I bet I would. Gives me a lift just knowing all of you think about me so often. Comparing lurid details, I suppose."

Julie was silent. Tybalt had a mole on his cheek. She had never noticed it before, and discovering the small detail about him made her feel warm and tingly. The force of the emotion generated by him was like a strong physical presence, and Julie felt as if she could grasp it. She knew he would kiss her, and when the sudden pressure of his mouth came down on hers she eagerly met his lips. For a few moments the sun and the wind, the packed earth beneath them, melted away; there was only Tybalt. He smelled of shaving cream and fresh air, of heat and sun-warmed wool. This was just the way Julie had always imagined it would be in her fantasies, when all ended in a rosy cloud of happiness. Then from somewhere far away she heard his urgent words in her ear. And her rosy cloud evaporated. "What did you say?"

"Oh, come on, Julie. Stop playing hard to get. Girls who accept weekend invitations know the ropes."

Shock radiated through her body, her lovely dream world shattered. Mustering her strength, she struggled to free herself from his grasp. Laughing, thinking this was some tantalizing game, Tybalt let her go.

"Well, you're skittish, I'll say that for you." He laughed, lazily surveying her as she stood above him. His breathing was shallow, and though he pretended humor, Julie could not mistake the anger coloring his face.

"How dare you think I'm like that!" she yelled, swinging at him with the first thing that came to hand: a switch of dried grasses.

Shielding himself from her onslaught, Tybalt covered his face. But not in time. She caught his cheek with the stinging lash of the grass, drawing blood. Surprised, he put up his hand, wiping the trickle of red. "Satisfied?"

"You deserved it," Julie snapped, cramming her hat low on her head and clutching her coat around her in protection. She scrambled away from him, shaking and fighting tears, then broke into a run. Here the track was fairly smooth, and she felt safer now. Footsteps crunched behind her and she increased her pace. It was foolish to think she could outrun him. He overtook her, seizing her arm and swinging her abruptly to face him. Fright and betrayed emotion made her sob. They stared at each other, Julie trying hard to see through the blur of tears. He was angry, his wide mouth set tight, his eyes cold. Blood had dried along the slash, and for a treacherous moment she felt remorse.

"Now what?" he demanded.

For the first time in her life Julie used a woman's escape from questioning. Not stopping to wonder if it would work with this man, she burst into a flood of tears. He resisted a moment longer, then his arms came around her and he cradled her wet face against his chest.

"Sorry. It won't happen again. Come on, don't cry. Surely you won't fault a guy for trying?"

She could hear the smile in his last statement, and blinking, she looked up, relieved to see the anger gone. He was the old Tybalt. "I suppose I'm partly to blame for coming with you in the first place, especially knowing all about you," Julie said darkly.

Tybalt grinned. "Hey, you make me sound like Bluebeard."

"Casanova, maybe."

Now they were both laughing, and he dabbed her eyes with a handkerchief. "You're really great, Julie."

"Thanks."

When he left her in the corridor outside her room, Julie was almost glad of the quarrel, even if she had been briefly afraid of him. Her relationship with Tybalt Shaw had climbed to a new plane. Now she felt more sure of herself. And of him.

The bedroom waited in all its faded splendor, the decaying aroma of mustiness mingling with gas in an unpleasant perfume. Julie threw her coat over the bed. The old scarf the dog had found tumbled from her pocket. There was a ragged name tape on the edge, and out of curiosity she brushed off caked mud and saw the name Deanie Jones. Though Julie was not sure why, she chilled at the discovery. After a few moments' reasoning with herself, she decided it was not so unusual for a girl's scarf to be in the woods, even that girl. "Grow up," she snapped to the empty room. Perhaps Deanie had not been as averse to Tybalt's plans as she. The girl had been a loner, and older than the other students. Julie's own rather prim moral upbringing had censured Deanie's lifestyle, ruling out much pity when news of the campus attack circulated. Probably deserved it, she could hear herself saying to Dottie over the morning paper. Then, when news of Deanie's death surfaced, they had agreed it was unfortunate, but not surprising. Smug and complacent fool! She had not been tempted by Tybalt then. Safe in the uninspired knowledge of Howard's romantic encounters, Julie had passed judgment on Deanie Jones from her own lofty pinnacle. This afternoon the edifice had been in danger of crashing.

A sudden bumping at the door made her heart skip a beat. The noise was followed by a whine: Caesar had come to call.

When she opened the door, the big black dog raced inside the room. At once he spotted the scarf, his morning trophy. "Oh, no, you don't." For some reason Julie did not want him to destroy the evidence. Evidence! Oh, boy, she was sounding like a detective yarn. Deanie's death had been a suicide; the case was settled. Policemen had no interest in Deanie's moral fall from grace. If Julie found her whole wardrobe in the Avon House woods, what difference would it make?

Denied the pleasure of his find, Caesar leaped at the bed, nosing her coat, snuffling and snorting in the pocket where his prize had been.

"Bring those back, you crazy dog," Julie

yelled as the dog pulled her gloves from the bed and charged toward the open door. He was gone in a flash, and she stumbled after him. Round the corner he sped, his claws skidding on the varnished wood.

"Of all the dumb things," she shouted, more for her own benefit than Caesar's, who was delighting in the new game. He headed for the stairs to the attics. Thinking to capture him on the staircase, Julie was surprised by his bounding agility as he took the treads two at a time. It was even darker up here, but Caesar made so much noise, scrabbling and snorting, that she had no difficulty in following him. He stopped at the end of a corridor, trapped in a dead end.

"Bad boy," she gasped, out of breath as she pounced at the squirming black body. Fortunately she was not afraid of dogs, or the Labrador's large mouth and formidable teeth would have been a barrier. Distastefully she retrieved her gloves, wet with saliva.

Thinking it was time for another game, Caesar skittered a few yards down the corridor, crouching and waiting for her to pursue him. She laughed at his foolishness and lunged halfheartedly as, with a yelp of joy, Caesar turned sideways, skidding toward a door that flew open before the onslaught. The dog leaped in surprise, scrabbling to a stop, and he whimpered alone in the dark unfriendly room.

Julie went to his rescue, wondering why she got herself into such silly situations. And feeling sorry for him, too. Anyone would think she had raced off with Caesar's gloves instead of the other way around.

"It's all right, silly boy. Here I am. Come on."

Julie reached around the door for the light switch. When it came on, the light shone murky yellow. This room, like most of the upper part of the house, had the odor of decay. Years of dust lay on everything. Caesar groveled over the floor, making a clean patch as he wagged toward her. Thank goodness this wasn't her room. Some poor soul must have stayed here, though, for there was a single hospital bed made up with sheets and a blanket. Who would want to sleep up here in the dark recesses of this ugly mansion?

Perhaps it had been the punishment room for disobedient servants in days gone by. A suitcase on a wooden crate caught her attention, and she pressed the clasp, wondering if someone were actually staying here now. The case was dusty, too, but not like the rest of the furniture. This was only a recent accumulation, while the thick cobwebs festooned in the corners looked years old. Caesar whined at her feet, suddenly uneasy. Julie glanced behind her but heard and saw nothing. The suitcase held a woman's clothing, such as someone her own age might use. Perhaps old Gerald kept a secret girl friend up here. It was an amusing thought. There was even a small prescription bottle among the underwear. Julie absently turned the label around to read the name, and she gasped in shock: the pills had belonged to Deanie Jones.

Caesar yelped excitedly as a footstep creaked in the doorway. In guilt Julie flung the capsules inside the case and closed the lid. Whoever was coming might not have noticed she was prying.

"Oh, it's you, my dear." Sarah Brookham walked inside the room, her sharp eyes darting about, taking everything in. Caesar slunk away at her sharp command.

"That nutty, silly dog ran off with my gloves. He really led me a chase," Julie explained brightly, hoping Sarah had not seen her looking in the suitcase.

"He's such a nuisance. Well, come down, we've been waiting for you. Lunch is growing cold. Tybalt said you should have been in your room, but when I went to fetch you, of course, you were gone."

"Sorry. I didn't know you were waiting," Julie apologized, watching as Sarah turned the key in the lock and pocketed it.

"We usually keep these rooms locked. That dog would make a shambles of them if he had a chance. I've warned Gerald about him, but, as you've probably noticed, he's not quite responsible at times."

They proceeded downstairs, Julie feeling uncomfortable in Sarah's presence. There was something unpleasant about the woman. Although she had a carefully practiced smile, it was as if only her mouth smiled, while her eyes remained hard and cruel. At the foot of the stairs Sarah paused, turning to look earnestly at Julie, her large cool hand resting on her arm.

"I'm going to be very blunt. Do you imagine Tybalt to be in love with you?"

Taken aback by the abrupt question, Julie gulped. "No," she said.

Some of the tension left Sarah's face. "I'm so glad you're sensible. Most of the girls he brings here are not. Tybalt does seem to attract a mixed bag of females. Most of them are hungry for money. And he's not hard to take along with it."

"We're casual friends, nothing more."

"Great. That's the only relationship he understands. Tybalt, bless him, is too much in love with himself to take any girl seriously. After all, he's quite a knockout in the looks department. If I were a few years younger, I'd fancy him myself," Sarah added with a sly wink, ushering Julie through the hall to the dining room.

Sarah's personal questions, coupled with the discovery of Deanie Jones's suitcase, robbed Julie of her appetite. Though she had no actual reason for her suspicions, her intuition told her something was dreadfully wrong. However upset Deanie had been when she left Avon House, she surely would not have gone without her suitcase. Even if she did not need the clothing, she would have wanted the medicine. And why had she been housed up there in the dusty attic? Sarah Brookham could probably have answered Julie's questions, but Julie knew that if she asked them she might learn nothing, and at the same time she would betray her own suspicions. She did not know if it was her imagination, or whether Tybalt's aunt already viewed her differently since their conversation, or even since Julie's discovery of the suitcase upstairs. At any rate, she might not have acted as casually as she thought she had.

Chapter 4

Julie lay wakeful in the heavy gray dawn. In a few minutes the Chinese gong would boom loud enough to wake the dead. Though she knew the hour of rising was inevitably approaching, she did not get out of bed; it was far too uncomfortable scurrying about this tomblike room without adequate heat. After the first few hours in this house Julie had already made up her mind never to grumble about the asthmatic floor furnace in her rented duplex again. Even the trainlike chugging and wheezing voice of that ancient contraption would be welcome in the drafty caverns of Avon House. Tybalt had certainly chosen well when he likened this house to a mausoleum.

Tybalt. The thought of him made her smile. Now that she knew him better, he did not seem so glamorously unapproachable. She had decided the reason he was so successful in his romantic life was because he had the girls buffaloed. They all felt obligated to please him, whatever his demands, in order to hold his attention. Baloney!

The muffled boom of the gong rocketed her into action. Pulling on her pink striped sweater set and black slacks, Julie brushed her long hair smooth and let it hang loose down her back. No reason not to play up one of her most glamorous assets, she thought with a smug smile as she went out into the corridor.

Tybalt's admiration was worth it. Though the flowing locks drifted over her face and into her eyes, his admiring glances cast in her direction made that unimportant. But every time she remembered that red scarf, or the suitcase upstairs, her joy turned slightly anemic. What did it matter? Deanie Jones was dead and Sandi Burns was out of the running. At the moment the only woman worth looking at in Tybalt's eyes was herself.

Another, less pleasant spin-off of her romantic looks this morning was Merky's heightened interest. At first Julie thought he really must have something in his eye, until she decided he was actually winking at her. The discovery made her want to giggle, and she had to hide her laughter by feigning interest in the newspaper that Sarah thrust in her hand.

"Look at that. A girl was attacked last night in Winton."

Though she saw little reason for Sarah's concern, Julie grew uneasy as she read the article. A girl coming home from work near the junior college had been attacked by an unknown assailant. Julie paled at the memory of the Smith College scare these past few months. "How far is Winton?" she asked.

"About a thirty-minute drive. Why?"

She met Tybalt's eyes, very bright this morning, gray like brook water. "Just asking."

Merky smiled and patted her arm, his lingering hand uncomfortably moist. "You're safe here, Julie. It's just some local masher."

"I take it we were all in our beds at twelve last night," Sarah finished, referring to the article for the time of the attack. "No one had an urge for doughnuts, did they?"

They looked from one to the other. Gerald Brookham, who had been silent up till now, chuckled at her words. "Come now, Sarah, there are thousands of ripe young men in Winton. Why should you suspect one of us? Too many trashy novels, my dear."

Sarah flushed brick-red at his scathing comment. "I thought I heard a car leave before midnight and return about one."

"In this driveway?" Tybalt asked with interest.

"Yes. Well, if no one left, I'm probably mistaken," Sarah finished lamely, glancing toward her husband, who purposely buried his nose deeper in a financial magazine.

Surely Sarah did not suspect him of the assault! Julie glanced from one to the other, picking up tension in the air, which made her uncomfortable. A few minutes later Sarah excused herself from the table.

Later, when she was finishing a cup of coffee beside the wide Gothic bay windows, Julie saw a figure hurrying along the path to the woods. It could have been anybody, but from the height and the purposeful movement to the dark-swathed form, she knew it was Sarah.

"Want to take a walk?" Tybalt asked.

Julie hesitated, and then she saw his understanding smile.

"Only a walk. No fast-paced romantic adventures. Promise." The smile he flashed melted her reserve, and she nodded.

The sun was out, but the wind was still cold. Julie pulled her car coat closer, trying to keep the wayward closings fastened as the wind frisked with the wooden toggle buttons.

Tybalt made small talk, something never difficult for him, yet when he carried on such a frothy, meaningless conversation, Julie could not help wondering if it were only for her benefit, if his heart were not really in it. His eyes seemed far away, as if he looked over and through her to some distant goal.

"You don't have to talk if you don't want to," she said at last. "Being quiet suits me."

His breath rasped a moment in surprise; then he grinned, patting her arm in thanks. Together they scaled the outcropping of gold-brown rocks near the mouth of the cave, neither mentioning the icy, beckoning crevice yawning blackly behind them.

"There's a heck of a view on the point. Want to see?"

Julie followed him up the treacherous path, glad of his helping hand as she stumbled on the rutted, rock-scarred ground. His gloved hands spread warmth through her own, and she unconsciously squeezed his fingers as he turned toward her at the summit of the path.

"Now, wasn't that worth it? Looks like something from a travelogue."

Julie agreed as she scanned the expanse of water, her free hand to her eyes to shield the sun. The lake was walled by craggy, pine-dotted slopes mingled with scrub oak. Some of the browned leaves still waved forlornly from the tree branches, untidy beside the more majestically clothed evergreens. Underground springs froze between the rocks, ending in cascades of thick icicles sparkling diamond-bright in the sun. It seemed as if they were miles from civilization overlooking an untamed land.

"Hey, this makes me feel like one of the pioneers," Julie gasped in wonder, not afraid today to voice her own thoughts.

"Yes, sure does. I really missed a lot not being born then."

"You! Traipsing across country in a covered wagon is the last thing I'd picture you doing."

"Well, people have been known to be wrong. Let's sit down."

Tybalt indicated a shelflike protrusion in the rock free of moisture. The chill radiated along her spine and she shivered, though he did not seem to notice the cold.

"Were you serious about wanting to live in the last century?" she asked at last, breaking the silence.

"Not just the last century, any century but this," Tybalt replied. "Gerald feels the same way, but since he imagines himself back in Shakespeare's time, that satisfies him. That's really the reason I turned to acting, to escape to the past, but it's not enough, not at Smith College anyway, though I doubt if I'd ever be good enough to go anywhere else. I'm a perfect candidate for a time machine."

"There's still plenty of adventure to be had today."

"Yeah, for some people. Not here, though. Living at Avon House, spookiness notwithstanding, is dull as ditch water."

"What about all the willing females who people the ivy-covered halls of Smith College?" Julie asked with sarcasm. "Aren't they exciting enough for you?"

Tybalt gave her a curious smile, his mouth appearing frozen above his gleaming teeth. Then the smile vanished, changing his face to that of a stranger. "You think you've got me all figured out, don't you?"

"You're not that hard to understand," Julie admitted, feeling rather smug in her knowledge.

"How wrong you are." His mouth turned bitter, and he seemed far older than the Tybalt she thought she knew.

"What do you mean, wrong? You are the typical heartthrob, God's gift to women, and so forth. What's there to be wrong about?"

"Some people see me like that, if I want them to," he agreed, his brow furrowed as he gazed across the sun-sparkled lake. "Inside I'm somebody else."

"Now, you're not going to tell me you don't like being Merky's nephew and the famous Gerald Brookham's handsome grandson. Come off it!"

"I hate being merely Tybalt of the Charming Smile."

Julie drew in her breath in surprise at the anger in his face.

"Sometimes I'm so restless I know exactly what all those poor creatures feel like in the zoo. I'm so caged I feel that if I don't get out I'm going to explode."

"Well, I can sympathize there. I went through a few years of that myself."

"Went through it? Does that mean you're over it?"

"Not completely," Julie admitted with a smile. "I have relapses at times."

He turned toward her, his expression still serious, so unlike his usual devil-may-care attitude. "Maybe it's being so typecast that gets to me," he began intently. "I don't know. The thing that eats me the most is that I haven't seen what's around the next bend or what's over the hill. There may be something great out there waiting for me, and I can't wait to find it. When my mother died, I was hitchhiking in Turkey. Of course, Gerald wanted me to come back. Seeing that I depend on him for my daily bread, what else could I do? I enrolled at Smith in the fall term."

He took a pack of cigarettes from his pocket and offered her one. He lit her cigarette and grinned at her serious face.

"It's a real kick in the head being rich, isn't it? Don't get me wrong, I'm not complaining. Gerald's been great to me. I couldn't ask for better. It's just that old wandering spirit. Maybe someday I'll have seen enough to get it out of my system."

His revelation made Julie do some serious thinking of her own. Her once-active desire to travel had been shelved out of necessity; now there was little to stop her. Her parents would not miss her acutely if she went abroad, that was certain. "You know, you've given me an idea."

"A sane one, I hope."

"Well, I don't know how sane it is, but it's thought-provoking, as the journalists are wont to say. There's a couple of overseas-job leaflets on the bulletin board at Smith. You may have given me the needed courage to apply for something. You never know."

"What about your folks?"

"That's something I haven't explained in detail to you — it's too painful. In a nutshell, Mom remarried, and her new husband can't cope with competition."

Tybalt pulled a face. "So what! You haven't lost much. Your mother probably still feels the same about you. If she's happy with Mr. Right, I guess you can always work out a compromise — a darned sight easier to establish on paper, believe me."

"You sound as if you're speaking from experience."

Tybalt managed a smile. "Am I! My father, Gerald, and I qualified for fights of the week when I lived at Avon House. After I left, things smoothed out. Of course, I did some growing up, I'm big enough to admit that. Yet in our case absence definitely made the heart grow fonder."

"You've given me some inspiration for my own problem. Thanks."

"You're welcome." He leaned toward her, and Julie did not move away. When his mouth brushed hers, it seemed right and good. For a moment she rested her head against the curly sheepskin collar of his coat, drawing comfort and strength from the warm pulsing life of him.

"Ever been in love?" he asked, startling her.

Julie shook her head. "No. Have you?"

Inside the thick coat Tybalt shrugged his shoulders, and the sheepskin tickled her face. "I've kidded myself a few times."

"Haven't we all."

Tybalt tightened his arm around her waist, but there was no urgency to the action. "If you ever feel like pretending again, keep me in mind," he whispered, his voice husky.

"Sure. You'll be the first to know."

On the descent Julie stopped at the cave, fascinated by the waiting darkness, as if some force drew her inside. Not at all happy with that idea, she shivered, deliberately stepping away from the temptation.

"Not that again," Tybalt said. "I'll definitely not go for a tour of the old family caves. They give me the creeps."

"It might be fun. Don't tell me you're afraid," Julie challenged, a gleam in her eye.

"Not afraid, just not interested," he replied, but the good humor had left his voice. "Come on. We'd better be going."

Smarting at his changed mood, Julie wished he wouldn't get so uptight about that stupid cave. That must be some romantic memory he had, or could it be that he was really afraid? Fearless though Tybalt seemed, it was often foolish things that made the bravest soul cringe.

"Sorry. I'm not addicted to caves, just curious."

"For what it's worth, my advice is to stay out of it. If you crack your head on a stalactite, or a stalagmite, or whatever, no one's going to know a thing about it. If you don't fancy languishing away on Cave Point, don't explore by yourself. Okay?"

Julie agreed, but reluctantly. Somehow the more he said against the place, the more it fascinated her. A curious, perverse streak obviously ran through her nature.

They returned to the house to find preparations under way for the evening dinner party. Mouth-watering smells wafted from the kitchen in the rear of the house. Tybalt left Julie in the library and went to answer his grandfather's request for an audience, his lip curling in scorn at the old-fashioned summons on a white card left in the silver tray by the door.

"Formal, what?" he joked in his best English accent, then, grinning at her surprise, he sprinted upstairs.

Julie wondered if she could do something constructive in the kitchen, though she did not fancy helping that grumpy maid. Maybe she could assist Sarah to ease the boredom. When Tybalt came back, she would mention it to him.

Wandering around the library, Julie found that the dusty titles on the packed shelves failed to attract her. The lights were so dim in here, filtered as they were through stained-glass windows, she wondered how anyone managed to study. The sun had gone behind a cloud, and the wind tossed the branches outside the windows, tapping them against the panes, the whispering, half-dead foliage sounding like voices beyond the glass. Rousing herself from her imagery, Julie could not prevent an icy shiver from creeping down her spine, or her skin from prickling as creaking boards outside the door heralded someone's approach. It could be Tybalt returning, but somehow the steps did not sound human.

With bated breath she watched the door move slightly inward, as if someone waited on the other side. Tension knotted her fists, choking her throat. Then, before her startled eyes, a black furry avalanche entered the room panting and wagging. A little scream of frightened relief escaped her lips as she collapsed into the nearest chair.

"You nutty dog! You'll give me a heart attack yet," she gasped when she found her voice. Caesar wagged and groveled unceasingly. At last Julie understood the reason for his unending delight: she was wearing her coat. "I've already been for a walk. We can't go again."

Caesar ignored the word "can't." He charged to the door and waited for her, looking back with doleful eyes. With a sigh she got to steadier feet, laughing as she remembered the absolute moment of fright before he made his noisy appearance. Fancy a dog skulking around doors like that, creeping about scaring folks. This pooch had to be part human!

The wind buffeted her head, and she drew the hood of her car coat snugly about her ears, clutching the fabric together as they raced toward the woods. Caesar brought her a stick to throw, and to her amazement he actually brought it back, seeming to enjoy the game of fetch and carry. Thank goodness there was the dog; at least he brought some lively interest into the mausoleum. She smiled as she used the word, deciding it would be her future reference to Avon House.

Caesar was more obedient today, Julie was surprised to find as he trotted patiently at her side. His new behavior lasted only until the cave came in sight; then he bolted for the dark interior to explore.

Recalling the episode here with Tybalt, Julie turned her back on the cave. Her feelings for him ran hot and cold. Sometimes she could almost hate him for his insufferable conceit, for assuming that all girls would fall in submission at his feet, for thinking she was like the others who had been here. Then at other times she could think of little more than his charming smile and the hot touch of his mouth on hers. The inner man revealed this morning had surprised and pleased her. Tybalt's thoughts and dreams fleshed out the too-perfect shell he presented to the world.

"Here, boy, come back, time to go," she called, managing her best whistle for the dog, who could be heard scrambling over rocks to do her bidding. Pleased with himself, Caesar reappeared, something clutched in his mouth.

"Now what have you found, you big

scrounge?" Julie laughed as she picked up the prize Caesar deposited at her feet. It was a wallet, the leather partially chewed and slimy to the touch, as Caesar's treasures proved to be. "Ugh, you really are a gross dog, you know that, don't you?" she complained with a grin, while Caesar wagged with pleasure at her assumed compliment. The wallet held a number of identification papers, and she opened it to a driver's license. The name on it was Sandi Burns. Good Lord, she thought with a stab of hurt and jealousy, was this another token of a lovely afternoon spent up here with Tybalt? He was despicable.

On the way back to the house she fumed as she pictured Tybalt and Sandi, Tybalt and Deanie, Tybalt and Julie — but there the picture changed. There would be no Tybalt and Julie to add to his scorecard. This was it. It was just as well she had learned about him before it was too late. Trying to feel satisfied with her sensible deductions, Julie hugged her arms around her body in an effort to lessen the cold that seeped through her coat to chill her limbs. And sadly she realized that whatever lies she took comfort from, it was already too late.

"Morning." A voice came from the shadows by the boathouse, and Julie jumped. Caesar wagged his tail and yapped in greeting at the shabbily dressed man who appeared on the path. Julie took him for a gardener since he carried a shovel.

"Oh, hello, you startled me," she said, ill at ease and conscious of the man's leer. He stooped, his long arms dangling apelike, his gray work clothes soiled with earth.

"Startled you! Sure didn't mean to. Just going to polish the car. It's a pretty. Want to look at it?"

Julie was inclined to say no, but there was something peculiar about his smile that made her change her mind. It would not hurt, and Caesar was here to protect her; besides, this was too lonely a spot for her to want to cross this man. His mannerisms made her wonder if he was mentally responsible, for his hands jerked involuntarily, like those of a puppet; when he spoke there was a slur in his speech, and when he was not speaking, his mouth hung slack, the lower lip red and wet.

Inside the garage it was cold and dark; even with the door open the deep shadows were black and frightening. Julie tried to keep away from him, but the man edged closer.

"Pretty car," he said, patting the sleek green body of the small sports car. "Pretty girl," he added slyly.

Julie smiled, edging toward the door and freedom.

"Want to take a ride in it? I can drive it if I want."

"No, thanks. I have to get back now." She quickened her step. "It was nice meeting you."

"We didn't really meet. You haven't introduced yourself."

"I'm Julie."

"I'm Arthur — Arthur Pence."

"Well, I'm pleased to meet you, Arthur. Now I really have to go." Charging for the expanse of open door, Julie grabbed the dog's collar, propelling him with her. Once outside, she broke into a run. The thought of riding with Arthur in that sports car with its checkered seat covers and big tasseled pillows on the back seat made her nauseated. His admiration for her was probably just as genuine as Tybalt's, but there was a tragic difference between them.

She was still shuddering as the house came into view, near-nightmares of a romantic interlude with Arthur receding comfortingly to the background. For once she found she did not even mind the tall, forbidding gables and twisted chimneys of Avon House, for it meant safety and habitation. And snapping her fingers at Caesar, she charged toward the house, the dog racing ahead.

Tybalt met her at the door, noting her startled expression and the sheer relief when she gripped his arm. "Hey, what's wrong? Seen a ghost?"

"No, just a creep with romantic notions."

Tybalt grinned but did not question her further. He stooped to fondle the dog's head before leading him toward the stairs. "Gerald's been looking for him. We couldn't imagine where he'd sneaked off to."

"Sorry if I spoiled anybody's plans."

"That's okay."

The more Julie thought about her morning find, the more she grew apprehensive. There was something going on here that did not add up. First Deanie's suitcase upstairs and her scarf in the woods, now Sandi's billfold in the cave. Maybe the scarf and the suitcase could be explained away. Deanie was dead; she had no further use for them. Sandi's billfold was different. She needed her driver's license. Had something happened to her? Was that why she had not accompanied Tybalt on this trip? Nonsense! Julie told herself with a grin. Sandi could have lost the billfold, or Caesar could have stolen it.

Here in the back of the house it was very quiet. As Julie walked toward the living room, hoping to thaw some of the chill from her limbs, she heard a bell ring in the distance. It sounded like a phone, but Sarah said they had none, so it was probably an appliance bell or a timer from the kitchen.

Standing with her back to the blazing fire, Julie sighed with pleasure as the warmth penetrated her black slacks. Her mysterious finds were not the only strange things about this weekend at Avon House. How about the report of that girl who had been attacked, and Sarah's reaction to it? She might as well have accused someone at the table of being involved by saying she had heard a car in the driveway at that hour. Yet what if she *had* heard a car leave and return? What if the campus attacker were here under the same roof?

"That's settled."

Julie looked up to find Tybalt crossing the room. "Hi."

"You really are a sucker. Ignore the old mooch. Caesar will run you ragged if you indulge him every time he wants a bit of excitement."

His words were half joking, and Julie smiled. "I'm a soft touch. Poor guy, I know what he feels like hanging around the house."

Tybalt grinned and patted her hair. "How about an exciting game of checkers? It's as exotic as we can get."

They set up the board beneath the windows, pushing an occasional table in place for the game. He won the first game because Julie could not keep her mind on the board. Visions of Deanie and Sandi kept popping into her head. Had Tybalt kept Deanie here in the attic while they shared a secret affair? She watched him covertly, wondering what hidden secrets he chose not to reveal. His heavy-lidded eyes flicked to hers a moment inquiringly, and she looked away. Why did he have such an aversion to the cave? Was it only because it was dark and dangerous, or was there another, far more sinister reason why he did not want her to explore the clammy recesses of Cave Point?

Plucking up courage to voice her suspicions was hard. They played a third game of checkers, and Julie knew he was growing bored. A burst of laughter from another part of the house distracted his attention. Girls' voices and scuffling steps passed the library door, bringing a smile to his mouth and curving his lips in a half-scornful, half-amused expression as he said, "That must be Merky playing hide-and-seek."

"Are you serious?" Julie was surprised by his statement.

"Sure. Didn't you know he's quite a chaser?"

"No. Well, at least not since his marriage," she said, recalling the soulful glances and chance handclasps bestowed on attractive girls in Merky's classes.

"My, you're really an old-fashioned girl," Tybalt observed, his voice low and almost awestruck. "You really believe that 'forsaking all others' bit, don't you?"

There was no scorn to his words, yet Julie found her cheeks reddening uncomfortably. "There are still a few of us left."

"Don't get sore. In a way I suppose you should take it as a compliment, in view of the new morality and everything. Go on, I'm teasing. I keep forgetting you're so serious about life. You'll have to get used to me."

"After yesterday do you still expect us to become accustomed to each other?" Julie asked in surprise, lowering her eyes from his direct gaze.

Ruefully Tybalt fingered the angry slash on his cheek. "You pack quite a wallop, Miss Virtue. But I guess I can learn to live with it."

His hand was soft on her neck, and Julie felt the delicious thrill of his touch, neary succumbing to the temptation of romance before the picture of that dark cave swam into view. She blinked. "Is the cave one of the scenes of your conquests? Is that why you don't want me hanging around there?"

Tybalt took his hand away. "Conquests? I'd hardly call them that. Besides, only a freak would fancy an icy cave in November. Aren't you getting carried away?"

"Whenever I mention going there, you seem to try to convince me to keep away."

"Well, it's pretty dangerous after all. And, as you said, there are only a few of you old-fashioned girls still around. I wouldn't want to decrease the number." With that he blew her a departing kiss, leaving her to brood over the half-empty checkerboard.

A few minutes later Julie saw him race past the window, chasing a girl with flying yellow hair along the terrace. A ball hurtled through the air, and several others joined the couple playing tag football on the wide lawn. Defying the brisk wind that sent leaves swirling to the grass, the laughing, energetic group charged toward the garages and out of sight, followed a moment later by a grinning Merky in a red sweatsuit. The ensuing silence seemed to press in on her, and Julie shuddered. The girls must be from the adjoining theatrical colony. She could have joined them, no one had excluded her from the impromptu game, yet no one had invited her to play, either, least of all Tybalt. And he still had not satisfied her curiosity about the cave. She desperately wanted to believe him, wanted him to remain as glittering as his former image, but somehow, in light of her discovery, she would never feel quite the same about him again. What a miserable Thanksgiving this was turning out to be! Having gained the sought-after romantic gem of Smith College, she seemed to have lost him. But worse than that, she was becoming involved in a mystery that might not even exist. Deanie Jones's thin, tanned face seemed to haunt her with its sad, lonely expression. Was there more to Deanie's suicide than met the eye? Had it even been suicide? Uneasily Julie wondered if the answer to those questions was here at Avon House.

Chapter 5

An immense clap of thunder shook the walls, and Julie leaped at the unexpected noise. The dark paneling pressed in on her, and her footsteps quickened, the unfamiliar passages frightening in the gloom. She longed for some light. The lightning must have hit the power lines, for when she tried the switches on the wall, nothing happened. The thought of spending even a couple of hours at Avon House without electricity was shattering; if the dark stairs and shadowy nooks were nerve-racking yesterday, tonight would be that much worse. Perhaps Tybalt would take her home if she pleaded illness. The shabby rooms across the street from Smith College seemed particularly desirable at the moment.

"Got you!"

Julie cried out in alarm, then was relieved to find her trembling form pressed quickly against Tybalt's broad chest for comfort.

"You scared me to death. What on earth are you wearing?"

Metallic trim on his jacket scratched her hands as she gently pushed him away. The fabric felt like velvet. In the garish white light that flashed suddenly through the windows she realized he was wearing a stage costume of jewel-embroidered doublet and tights, a sword at his side glinting fire in the lightning.

"Pretty far out, don't you think?" He chuckled, turning before her and strutting a few paces. "Gerald says he wore it in London. He's got something for you, too."

"I'm comfortable in what I'm wearing, thanks."

"Oh, come on. Humor the old bird. He says tonight is really important to him. What can it hurt?"

What could it hurt? Julie asked herself later as she squeezed into a salmon velvet gown with a high waist and long sleeves gathered to form three puffs. Tybalt had been very persuasive, and it was just for fun. If Gerald Brookham wanted to create a few hours of illusion to comfort him in his retirement, why should she refuse to go along with it? It might be fun having everyone sitting down to the feast by candlelight attired in costumes from the past. It would be like stepping back in time. But although she knew it was a convincing argument, Julie could not wholly accept the innocence of the game. A sixth sense warned her of danger.

The dining room buzzed with chatter and laughter. Peering around the door, Julie was surprised to find a dozen people already seated at the long refectory table. From their youth and authentic stage costumes she guessed them to be students from Brookham's artist colony whom he had invited for the occasion.

"Come on, you're sitting by the host," Tybalt whispered, smiling at her surprise.

Even Tybalt seemed different now that he was dressed like this, Julie thought, watching him laugh with a girl in black satin. Everything seemed unreal. Though the steaming food on the table was definitely twentieth-century, it was hard to imagine this feast being bought at the neighborhood supermarket. Rather, it suggested wagonloads of produce from country estates, and spices and wines brought by merchant ships from afar. Then a girl seated opposite her destroyed the illusion; she reached in her purse for a compact to check her eye make-up, and Julie could have hugged the stranger for breaking the spell.

Turkey and ham steamed before her; mounds of potatoes and vegetables; silver trays of relishes; bread boards piled with crispy rolls, and at each place a sparkling Venetian goblet of ruby wine. Candies sputtered and dripped; beaded wax ran in streamers on the lace tablecloth. No one ate, and Julie realized the place beside her was empty. They were waiting for Gerald Brookham. He arrived a moment later, and she blinked to clear her vision. Though not an avid follower of Shakespeare, she could not have mistaken his identity, as the only painting she had seen of the writer sprang to life before her. A round of applause followed his appearance. Raising his glass, a young man in partial armor proposed a toast: "To our creator, the immortal Will Shakespeare."

Only then did Julie realize that every guest represented a specific character. Each person introduced himself. With a quip and a flourish Merky used his given name, reminding them of his rightful place in the cavalcade of characters. Following suit when their turn came, Julie and Tybalt did the same. All seemed in order, for Gerald nodded his approval.

Throughout the meal Julie was uncomfortably aware of her host's eyes on her, and when she raised her goblet of wine, he startled her by saying, "From such a cup did Juliet die."

Hastily Julie replaced the wine undrunk. At her side Tybalt smiled as he prodded her in the ribs, finding her dismay amusing. "He means my mother."

In horror Julie turned to him, seeing his eyes strangely metallic and bright. Had he drunk a little too much perhaps? "Your mother was poisoned?"

"Purportedly by her own hand. In this wacky family what else would you expect?"

"Oh, Tybalt, I didn't know. I'm so sorry."

"I'm over it now. They had a zany love pact, she and my father, or at least that's what Gerald claims."

"That's eerie. Just like Romeo and Juliet."

"Eerie and romantic and stupid," he snapped, draining his glass. Automatically a waiter, dressed in Elizabethan livery, stepped forward with a refill.

"Why did they do it?"

"It was after one of these weekend affairs. Mother apparently took an overdose of medicine, washing it down with wine. Sorry to destroy the image, but Dad shot himself. I guess if he had had the forethought, he would at least have done it the right way to please Gerald. Oh, and his name was Fred."

For the rest of the meal Tybalt was moody. Julie knew he was on his fourth glass of wine and that she had no right to attempt to limit his intake, but she fervently hoped he would not get drunk and leave her with these strangers. The other people ignored her, and she felt lonely and afraid. So Tybalt's mother had died after such a party. Though she did not ask, Julie knew instinctively that she must be sitting in her place at Gerald's side. Merky was on his other side, his wife beside him, attired as Lady Capulet in a jeweled net and dark green gown trimmed in gold. Julie gave her a couple of friendly smiles, but Sarah remained indifferent. What would take place tonight? Would this party also end in tragedy? It was easy to imagine violent deeds in this paneled room with the flickering candles, the rain lashing outside, and the lightning flashing between the curtains. These people were so unreal. The situation itself was unreal. For a panic-stricken moment Julie wondered if she was having a nightmare. After a suppressed gasp following a bruising self-pinch, no one faded away. She was awake, all right. No wonder Deanie Jones had been terrified during the play. In these surroundings, what else?

Uneasily she wondered what the other girl friends had thought about these eerie, fancy-dress dinners. "You said you brought other girls here. Did they like all this?" Julie asked carefully, wary of Tybalt's strange, wine-induced mood.

He pushed his dessert plate aside and clasped his hands, the knuckles growing white. "They were afraid. I told you that. Are you afraid?"

86

She lied and denied the emotion, though it took all her courage. Tybalt must not think she fell short of his expectations. "Did anything happen to anyone — besides Deanie?"

"What makes you ask that?" he snapped, turning toward her.

"I wondered, since they were afraid, what it was they feared."

"This house. The aura here. You must have noticed."

Noticed? It had been one of her first impressions!

"Old houses often feel spooky."

"This place is more than that. I wish I hadn't brought you."

"Why? Aren't I playing along with things?" Julie asked in disappointment. It had cost her so much to keep up a pretense, it was a shock to learn she was a failure.

"Oh, yeah, that's not what I meant. You're a pretty nice girl, not the usual sort I bring here. In the beginning you were just a girl —" He paused, clasping her hand beneath the cloth. "Shall we go back tonight?"

Julie gasped with delight at his suggestion. She had prayed he would offer to take her back, had wanted to ask, yet had been afraid of his anger. It was still important to impress him with her good qualities, whatever else she told herself.

"What's wrong with now?"

He smiled, and his change of expression made her heart lurch. "After Gerald's speech."

Julie glanced toward the host, who had scraped his chair back and stood with his hands clenched on the table. The conversation fell silent as everyone waited for his words.

"Dear, beloved characters, I have given birth to you, lived and loved through you, taken revenge and suffered pain, all played out for me by your actions. I salute you during this final meeting."

A murmur of dissent rippled around the table, but he held up his hand for silence. Watching him, Julie understood why Tybalt thought him crazy. This was more than the eccentric whim of an aging actor. Gerald Brookham really believed he was William Shakespeare. The others took it lightly, enjoying his patronage and enduring his idiosyncracies, but Julie saw that to their host this was reality.

"No, dear friends, it will be the last, though we shall not be denied some amusements." Gerald paused to wipe his eyes, whether in a theatrical gesture or from a genuine need, Julie was not sure. "I, unlike thou, am not immortal. My body is frail. My daughter Juliet and I have long enjoyed your company;

now, alas, it must end. The legacy will remain, to be disbursed by my surviving kin. He will be generous. Now, dear friends, I am very tired." Bowing, Gerald swept majestically from the room, his exit followed by a deafening crash of thunder that sent more than one heart fluttering with shock.

"What does he mean?"

Tybalt stood, ignoring the guests' murmured questions. From the puzzled expression on his face Julie discovered that he did not understand the speech, either. More bewildering than the words "final meeting" was Gerald's reference to his surviving kin — used in the singular. Surely both Merky and Tybalt were equal relatives.

Taking command of the situation, Tybalt smiled charmingly and thanked everyone for coming, then wished them a happy holiday. Disgruntled but well-fed, the guests departed, climbing aboard a couple of garishly painted vans parked in the driveway.

Julie watched from the doorway, finding the spectacle unreal as the Shakespearean-costumed players disappeared inside vehicles bright with rock-culture symbols.

Merky closed the door, avoiding Julie's gaze. There was something strange about his expression as he said, "Gerald wants us all in the living room. His announcement's going to make your hair curl."

Tybalt shrugged. Merky hurried away, skinny and stoop-shouldered in his striped hose and doublet. "First I'm going to check the basement fuses," Tybalt said with determination. "Something peculiar's going on. The gatehouse has lights."

Julie had not noticed, for she had been too intent on the departing guests. She shuddered as she waited for Tybalt at the head of the stairs. He made a peculiar sight in his powder-blue velvet costume, carrying a candle while he grumbled over the fuse panel.

"Well, what happened?" she asked as he came upstairs.

"You're not going to believe this."

"What?"

"The fuses are gone. Must be one of Gerald's ideas to impart some authenticity to the show. Anyway, now that everyone's gone home, perhaps we can have some lights."

Together they walked down the hall. At the door Tybalt pulled her back in the shadows as they heard Gerald's strong, resonant voice:

"No heir but you — or Tybalt. Perchance this time we shall rewrite the bard's work, dear Mercutio."

"Lord, he's really bananas tonight," Tybalt remarked, hesitating before he said, "You still want to go home, right?"

"That's the best idea you've ever had," Julie replied with relief.

"Okay, we'll hear him out, then leave. I'm sorry I brought you. Hopefully this won't be the last time. Maybe we'll be able to leave in time."

"In time for what? The storm's worse than it was before dinner." To punctuate her words, lightning flashed through the window and thunder rolled menacingly overhead.

"I didn't mean the storm." Tybalt's voice was tight, and something about his tone made Julie afraid.

"What, then?"

"I told you about Deanie. Do you remember the other two girls who were attacked? Each of them had been here before that happened. At first I didn't see any connection, then I knew it was too much of a coincidence. Bringing them here somehow marked them for attack. That's the real reason I'm sorry I brought you. After I quarreled with Sandi, you were the first likely substitute — sorry, Julie, but I have to be honest."

His words felt like a douse of ice water. Julie drew back from him. So there had been no admiration, no reason other than convenience for the invitation. And now, by accepting it, she had opened herself to peril.

"Knowing that, how could you do it to

me?" she whispered, trembling in the dark.

"Listen, I know it sounds callous, but I honestly didn't think about the attacks. I needed a girl for the weekend. It was no more than that. You were pretty . . . and, well, available."

Tears stung her eyes and she turned away. Tybalt's hand caressed her hair, and though she wanted to pull away entirely, she could not bring herself to refuse the only kind, human contact offered to her.

"Please take me home."

"Julie, that's how I felt *then*. Today you matter too much to me to be that casual."

She looked up at him in the gloomy hall, lit partially by the glow of leaping flames from the living room. He was so handsome in his romantic costume, so manly, the shadowed paneling making him seem part of a picture come to life. But when he kissed her, the warm pressure of his mouth was real.

"This is the way I feel about you now." Then he grinned, and seizing her hand, he marched boldly inside the living room.

Chapter 6

Gerald, Merky, and Sarah waited in the dim room, where now only a lone candle sputtered wildly. The scene made Julie shiver in her low-necked gown.

"Come, Daughter."

In dismay Julie held back. "I'm not your daughter," she gasped. "I'm Juliet Brown."

"Humor him. He's a dying old man," Merky hissed behind her, and she felt his fingers biting hard on her arm as he thrust her forward, until she lurched against the furniture.

Tybalt, warming himself at the hearth, did not hear the exchange. Julie shuddered at the crackling tension she felt in the room. Whatever this hair-curling announcement was going to be, she wished they would get it over with so that she could leave this musty tomb and its assorted cracked inhabitants. Gerald patted the scarlet velvet chair beside him, and warily Julie was seated.

"Tybalt and Mercutio, Lady Capulet and

Juliet, we lack a few characters for our masque, but for this scene it will suffice," he declared, the old resonance in his voice.

Julie wracked her brain for the part these characters were supposed to play, wondering what evil intention was brewing here. There would be no repetition of Macbeth, so at least that was a blessing, yet the spectacle presented for her might surpass Deanie Jones's unnerving experience.

Gerald leaned forward, his face appearing parchment-white and giving his fine-boned features the aura of approaching death. Could there have been truth to the speech in the dining room? Was it more than convincing dramatics?

"My doctor has given me no more than a month to live. It's something I've expected for some time. I don't want sympathy."

He did not get it. The circle of faces, lurid in the firelight, was attentive, and though Julie gasped at his surprising statement, she alone voiced her dismay. Tybalt accepted the words, his face grave. On Merky's face was a look of greed, the expression even more pronounced on the dark, slanted features of his wife. Even though she was not fond of Gerald Brookham, Julie was disgusted by their apparent joy at his impending death.

"There will be only one heir. Never could

stand that will-haggling. His name shall be decided in true thespian fashion by a duel. It's an irony that the two contestants should have such appropriate names. 'Tis a pity we are not in the midst of a hot afternoon in Verona, but some concessions must be made. After all, both Romeo and Juliet have served us in the past."

Tybalt stiffened at his words. Merky's eyes flashed anger and revenge. Now Julie recalled the scene in question: Mercutio and Tybalt had fought a duel in which Mercutio was killed. Surely this was not how Gerald intended to decide who would inherit Avon House!

"You're not expecting them to duel to the death!" she cried, leaping to her feet.

Gerald smiled. "Dear Juliet, stay calm. Your time has passed, for in this performance our scenes are crossed, our own hero and heroine dead before the final act."

Merky seized one of the swords from the display on the wall as, laughing, Tybalt drew the gleaming sham at his side.

"All right, Grandfather, to humor you."

They stepped to the center of the room while Gerald lit a tall candelabra and placed it on a side table. "Play on," he commanded grandly, returning to his chair.

Tybalt maneuvered himself into position.

"Come on, Merky, let's make it look good," he said in an undertone, winking at his uncle, who dashed straggling pale hair from his eyes as he made a few practice thrusts.

The garish scene that followed made Julie gasp. She had seen these two fence before, but with appropriate sham weapons on stage at Smith Hall. This unbelievable arrangement at the whim of an insane old man was entirely different. As they stumbled and weaved, an ominous truth began to make itself apparent. Merky was not acting. Tybalt knew it, too, she was sure, for his face tightened as he stared a moment in disbelief at his uncle, who slashed and cut with deadly determination.

"Stop it, both of you," Julie yelled, afraid for Tybalt's safety. Merky's sword, though probably blunt, was an actual weapon. To her dismay Sarah seized her with unexpected strength, pinioning her arms to her sides.

"Shut up, you little fool."

Julie was appalled. Was Sarah insane, too? Was she actually living her own role as Lady Capulet? "Let me go! If you won't try to stop them, I will. I think you're all nuts!" Julie shouted, struggling to be free.

"It's too late to stop them. Too much has already been done for this inheritance. You won't stop me now. Forget it. Besides, Tybalt doesn't care about you," Sarah hissed.

In fury Julie kicked her smartly in the shins, making Sarah recoil in pain and slacken her grasp. Seizing her opportunity, Julie bolted for the open door just as Tybalt stumbled, clutching his shoulder. Torn between helping him and going for assistance, she hesitated a moment too long, time enough for Sarah to grab her flowing pink skirt.

"I've killed him. You see, Father, I'm not such a failure after all!" Merky cried in triumph, his voice going high and squeaky.

To her surprise Julie saw Sarah's pale face crumble at the statement, her mouth quivering. The shock made her loosen her hold on Julie's gown. Her captive forgotten, Sarah ran to Tybalt's side, supporting him against her chest. In horror Julie watched them, finding the scene frighteningly bizarre, as if she had wandered into another century. First the duel, the participants in Renaissance costume, and now this woman, similarly garbed, sobbing over a wounded man. The most horrible part of it all was that Tybalt was the man.

Stifling a cry, Julie raced from the room, her mind in a whirl. Why was Sarah so concerned for Tybalt? Had her casual statement that she would fancy him herself if she were younger only been to put Julie off the trail? Surely Sarah could not be in love with him. But her grave concern indicated that she was.

"He's not dead! You couldn't even commit murder properly, you poor failure," Gerald's voice boomed forth with all its accustomed resonance, carrying to the drafty hallway, his scornful statement satisfying Julie's fears for Tybalt.

Steps creaked on the stairs, and with relief Julie saw the maid peering over the banisters. "Quick, we've got to get help. We need an ambulance. Tybalt's hurt."

The maid blinked sleepily at her urgency, not comprehending as Julie raced toward her, sobbing and stumbling over her gown. "Are you feeling all right?" the woman demanded, pulling her senses together as she modestly clutched her robe.

"Yes, I'm all right. Don't you understand, it's Tybalt. They fought a duel and he's bleeding."

The woman sighed in relief, shaking her head swathed in a mammoth curler cap bristling with rollers. "So you're another. We do get 'em. That Mr. Tybalt sure can pick winners. Mr. Brookham puts on such a good act, that's all. Too much imagination, you young girls, that's what it is."

"It's not an act. It's true. Tybalt's bleeding!"

"All right, if you insist. I'll go in and see," the woman sighed, reluctantly scuffling down the worn stair treads. "Get yourself a drink, honey. It'll steady your nerves."

Declining the woman's advice, Julie stumbled toward the kitchen where earlier she had heard what sounded like a phone. Her long skirts hampered her passage, so she lifted them around her knees as she ran to the back of the house. The kitchen was empty. To her delight she saw a phone, despite Sarah's assurance that they were not on the phone line. Her reasoning behind the lie was another mystery. Gulping air, Julie attempted to steady her voice before she spoke. Seeing no phone book and not knowing the police number, she dialed the operator. Just as the reply came over the receiver, hands grabbed her, snatching the phone from her.

"No way, Miss Nancy Drew." Sarah blocked the doorway.

"We must do something for him," Julie gasped, wishing she had not wasted precious time with the housekeeper.

"Don't worry, Tybalt's not dying. You forget I'm a nurse. Just a scratch. Needless to say, Merky couldn't mortally wound a frog."

Sighing in relief, Julie found her tired body relinquishing strength against Sarah's almost masculine arms. Had she imagined that glimpse of the other Sarah crouched over Tybalt? Had there actually been tears on her face, or was it merely a trick of the flickering light? Now the smooth porcelain flesh was unmarred, the dark eyes hard and bright.

"Thank you for helping him," Julie whispered.

"Well, I certainly didn't do it for you. I helped him for me."

Startled by Sarah's statement, Julie tried to pull away. "For you? What about your own husband?"

"Don't make me laugh. If you can compare Merky to Tybalt, you must need glasses," Sarah snapped. "No one in his right mind could do that."

"Why did you marry him, then? Wouldn't Tybalt have you?" The question hit home, Julie knew by the flash of temper and the renewed pressure biting into her arm.

"You don't need to make any stupid assumptions. No one cares what you think."

"I'm right, then, aren't I?"

Sarah's face turned dusky, and she pushed Julie toward the stairs. "Yes, but being right won't do you any good. Someone like you thinks they can have everything. College, youth, Tybalt too. You're just like all the other little girls he brought here. Tybalt needs a real woman, not some cutesy cheerleader."

"What about the others? What do you know about Deanie Jones?" Julie demanded

100

as she was propelled upstairs.

"I imagine she was a great friend of yours."

"I knew her."

"That one tried to be a little too clever for her own good. Poking, prying, trying to blackmail us. But I took care of that. Let that be a lesson to you."

"You killed her, didn't you? Her suicide was murder instead."

"Prove it," Sarah challenged, dragging Julie at breakneck speed around the curving banisters.

Though she wanted to resist, Julie had no will to fight her. As they ascended the attic stair the mystery of where she was being taken was solved; the cobwebby room awaited her. "What could Deanie know to blackmail you, anyway?"

Sarah fumbled for the key to the door among the cluster dangling from her chatelaine, part of her costume. Though Julie thought she would be able to wrestle free, Sarah proved tremendously strong. In a minute they were inside the cold, dusty prison.

"Oh, don't pretend, fishing for answers. Deanie told me she had a girl friend who knew everything. I've been waiting all month for you to show up."

"Look, Sarah, you've got the wrong person. I barely knew Deanie, honest. I barely even know Tybalt."

"Don't give me that," Sarah snarled, her face suffused with hatred. "I know Tybalt doesn't go for long hikes in the woods for the good of his health. You forget, I worked here for several years. I think I know him pretty well."

A moment later the key grated in the lock, and Julie was alone. She held her head, pressing her forehead in an effort to clear the muddled thoughts that whirled through her brain. What could Deanie Jones have known that was worth money to Sarah to keep quiet?

No one came to the room all night. Julie alternately dozed and called for help, her voice growing hoarse until she gave up the effort. Here at the top of the house, muffled in dust and clutter, her voice seemed powerless. There was a small window like a porthole in the far wall, and when it was light enough to see, Julie investigated this possible means of escape. The window was securely fastened with a padlock, but the hinge was very rusty; if she had a heavy object to batter it loose, she might be able to climb to safety.

When Sarah brought her food, she had almost given up hope of being found. The toast was cold and Julie thrust it aside.

"What's wrong? Don't you want your breakfast? The condemned man always has a final meal. I guess you don't read much," Sarah ended with a scornful laugh.

"You'd better let me go. My parents know I'm here. Then there's Tybalt —"

"Don't lose any sleep over him. I'll tell him you freaked out — that is the current vernacular, isn't it? He's used to that sort of thing. Deanie wasn't the first, you know. Poor boy, he has rather a bad track record. All losers."

"My parents," Julie persisted, growing desperate.

"Don't you remember, you told me you were alone," Sarah flashed in triumph. "Good try."

So she had. An inner warning told Julie to keep quiet about the implied statement; having contact with the outside world could be her ace in the hole. "You can't keep me here."

"Who says?"

"Sooner or later someone from Smith will make inquiries."

"How will anyone from Smith know you're here?"

"I left a note for my roommate," Julie lied, noting the surprise reflected on Sarah's face.

"So you decided to take off. It's all the same to her."

"She knows me better than that. My education is too important for me to do that."

"Tybalt will bear the story out."

"You've lied to him about me, haven't

you?" Julie gasped, wondering how he could take Sarah's word for the situation without making an investigation, without insisting on some proof. Yesterday they had been so close for a little while, she had thought their friendship firmly cemented by their exchange of ideas. And now the illusion was gone.

"Oh, come on, you're too good to be true." Sarah's laugh was heavy with scorn. "Easy come, easy go; that's Tybalt's motto, bless him. It certainly makes things easy."

"Things," Julie repeated suspiciously as Sarah moved toward her, the bare boards echoing with her heavy tread. "What kind of things?"

"There aren't going to be any more little fly-by-night romances ruining my plans. You have to go. It's nothing personal — you're not bad as girls go, I must admit."

"Thanks for nothing."

Sarah smiled as she collected the dishes. "Here's a thermos of hot coffee. Sorry I can't offer you central heat, but there's a couple of blankets in that chest. You can wrap up in those till I decide what I'm going to do with you."

Numbly Julie entertained wild thoughts of overpowering Sarah, or at least making enough noise and commotion to rouse someone in the house. She hesitated too long, and

Sarah turned back from the dishes.

"I'll be back later," she promised before disappearing through the door and locking it behind her.

A better idea than overpowering Sarah would be to open that window and yell to the first person who went by. Determined to succeed, Julie wobbled along the bed and rattled the window in its frame, praying for a miracle, but unfortunately the catch held, although one of the screws became loose in its hole. In desperation she looked about for a weapon. Sarah had removed the mystery suitcase, which Julie would have liked to investigate, taking all but a battered chest and the army cot on which she slept. With sudden inspiration Julie recalled a camping trip she had taken with the Girl Scouts, and the struggle she had had pushing the wooden laths through the canvas hems on the cots. Perhaps she could use one of those laths to pry out that faulty hinge.

Struggling with the weathered material, Julie managed to work the wood out, tearing the canvas in the process. Without supports she could no longer stand on the bed, so she pushed the chest beneath the window. The ends of the wood chipped and splintered until at last she succeeded in dislodging the hinge. Panting and gasping over her efforts, she did not notice the numbing cold that seeped around the poorly fitting window, adding to the refrigerated atmosphere of her prison. The second hinge yielded as she battered the corroded metal, and she flung the window open. It hung crazily lopsided from its pad-locked catch.

A sticky wetness trickled down her arm, and in surprise she found she had sliced her hand on the rusty metal. The cold had so numbed her fingers, she had noticed little beyond the jab when the wound was inflicted. Now it throbbed, pumping blood. Feeling sorry for herself, Julie sucked her injured hand, spitting out the unpleasant salty taste of blood. She tore a piece of bedsheet to make a bandage, growing apprehensive when she saw that as soon as the knot was made, the material was quickly stained red.

Perching on the chest, Julie hung in the window frame by her elbows, trying to hoist herself higher. An icy wind, tainted with wet earth and foliage, gave her an invigorating slap in the face. The agony in her elbows, coupled with the stinging throb of her bleeding hand, forced her to drop down for a breather, thumping hard upon the tin trunk and cursing its unyielding contours as she skinned her leg. At this stage a cup of hot coffee would be more than welcome.

Julie paused in the act of finishing the first steaming cup to consider how unlike Sarah it was to provide even this small luxury to add to her comfort. It was hardly the act of a jailor, unless — Hastily Julie spat back the hot liquid. How else would Sarah assure her cooperation? The coffee was surely intended to put her out of action until Sarah had her plans in order.

Angry at her own gullibility, Julie renewed her efforts at the window. Fortunately she was small. A larger person would have been hopelessly trapped. The trailing, slippery fabric of her stage gown was no help as she wiggled and wormed her way upward. Now she was far enough out so that she could not touch the chest when she strained her legs down. Inch by inch, she squeezed through the porthole, buffeted by the stinging wind, her hair flying loose. Her hands supported her, and she did not dare let go in order to remove the offensive flying strands.

At last, after a final tremendous heave, she tumbled through the opening onto a narrow catwalk on the roof. Swaying precariously, she crouched against the gable, clutching masonry and ivy tendrils, trying to get a handhold. She made the mistake of looking down; nausea and giddiness gripped her, sending the life-sustaining wall into wavering relief against an iron-gray sky. Sweat broke out clammily on her brow and upper lip while she held her breath to control the vigorous churning in her stomach.

Her eyes closed tightly, she waited for what seemed an eternity for the world to right itself, to be still and stop its dangerous, dizzy swaying. At last she tentatively opened her eyes to see huge slabs of masonry twisted with a network of brown ivy tendrils, the dark leaves spattered with bird droppings; but there was no longer that hypnotic sway, no further blurred vision. Forcing herself not to look down, Julie stood, clutching for a handhold among the weathered vines. Fearfully she worked her way along the gable, crawling painfully over broken tiles to reach a comparative haven in a nest of twisted chimneys.

Everything seemed so far away; the boathouses and garages looked like toys from here, the lake itself a small gray puddle. It was cold, and Julie huddled against the masonry where warmth and smoke exuded from a working chimney. Scuffling around in the ivy, she made a nest for herself, wedged safely between three chimneys, and settled down to think.

Chapter 7

When Julie opened her eyes it was dark. Starting up, she soon crouched down again, shocked to find she was still on the roof. Surely she could not have slept till nightfall, perched up here in a nest like a bird, yet overhead stars glinted, their brilliance obscured by heavy storm clouds. That was all she needed, another deluge while she was nesting on the roof. Laughing nervously at her predicament, Julie scrambled over the roof slates. She had to laugh; her only other alternative was to resort to hysterics, a state from which she was not far removed. Hysterics never solved anything, she reminded herself sourly as she reached the opposite side of the house, where she found matching gables. Moving about up here in the dark did not seem as bad as it had been in the light, for now she could not really see the drop below, and her passage was slow out of necessity, giving her a false sense of security. The windows were fastened. However, at the front of the house the style of the gable windows was different; here they were small, square, stained-glass panes. If she broke the glass, she could open the catch.

Julie struggled to pry a broken roof slate loose, rubbing her knuckles against the stone with her effort. Bashing repeatedly against the window, she was rewarded by a shattering splinter. In panic she stopped, the noise echoing in the silence until she was sure Sarah had heard it, for by now her captor must know she was free.

No one was roused by the sound. Hardly able to believe her good fortune, Julie squeezed back inside the house from which earlier she had worked equally hard to leave. What irony, she thought, laughing softly in sheer emotional relief. The small room was littered with storage boxes. The door was not locked. Julie crept into the passage, finding the house silent as a tomb. Surely she couldn't be the only one still here. What if Avon House were empty after the Thanksgiving holiday! If that was the case, she would be able to move about undetected. A muffled cough from one of the rooms soon dispelled her sense of security.

The one idea in her mind was that phone in the kitchen. At this hour no one should be there. It was a ray of hope. When she reviewed the events of the past days, she began to doubt her sanity. Such things couldn't happen in the middle of the Ozarks, but happen they had, or she was more ill than she thought.

The kitchen lay in darkness. Stealthily she lifted the receiver, relieved to hear the dial tone. She would call the police. Yet the delay waiting for the operator to connect her could be vital; then, after she spoke with them, she had no assurance that the local sheriff's office would consider her accusations seriously, coming as they did from so prestigious a location. At last Julie decided to call Smith College instead. Sandi Burns was an interested party, and she could certainly clear up a few mysteries if she was there.

Julie dialed the dorm number. Sandi knew Julie's reputation for levelheadedness. If she was convinced by her story, Sandi would go a long way to convincing the police. That is, if Sandi were still able to call. . . .

At last the impersonal voice of the operator came on. Trying to keep her voice barely above a whisper, Julie croaked the number. As she spoke she glanced behind her warily, startled by moving shadows over the kitchen wall. The moonlight was suddenly crossed by waving branches, and she sighed with relief as she heard the wind tossing the maple against the windowpane.

"Sandi Burns, please."

"Hi. Sandi's not here. This is her room-mate, Bev."

Julie searched her mind for the girl's identity, then remembered. Bev was also a cheerleader, statuesque and blondely attractive. "Bev, this is Julie Brown. You probably don't remember me, but we're both in Merky's drama group."

"Julie? Oh, sure, I know you. Dottie's pal."

Sighing with relief, Julie glanced about, making sure she was still alone. "Bev, where's Sandi?"

"Can you speak up? It sure is hard to hear you. Sandi's away for the vacation. I wouldn't be here myself except I picked up stupid chicken pox. Can you believe at my age —"

"Where's Sandi staying?" Julie cut in.

Bev hesitated. "Well, I guess it doesn't hurt to tell you. She's with her boy friend."

"Tybalt Shaw?" Julie gasped, her heart lurching with a sickening movement.

"Yeah, he's the one. Say, you still there? You sound odd. Are you in trouble or something?"

"Yes. And I need your help. Please listen, there's not much time. I'm the one here with Tybalt, not Sandi. If she's not there, and you haven't heard from her, she could be in danger." "Dead" seemed too brutal a word to use on the phone; besides, she really had nothing to go on.

Bev gasped, Julie's statement catching her by surprise. "You serious?"

"I wish I weren't. Merky's wife is up to her neck in whatever's going on here at Brookham's. Let me ask you this. Did Sandi know Tybalt's previous girl friend, Deanie Jones?"

"Sure, everyone knew her, or about her," Bev replied.

"I don't mean like that. I mean *really* know her. About what happened to her."

There was another pause. Then, in a frightened tone, Bev asked hoarsely, "She told you about it, too?"

Bev's unguarded statement told Julie what she wanted to know. Sandi was the one to whom Sarah had referred, the girl friend Deanie had taken into her confidence. "Did Sandi tell you any details?"

"Not much. Just about Deanie's relationship. And how she said she was going to get enough money out of them to set herself up. Sandi figured some of the answers from the start, but she had to be sure. It's nothing against Tybalt, but that's the reason she started dating him. She got a letter from Deanie that explains things. Anyway, how did you know?" Bev's tone had grown wary, afraid now that she had said too much.

"Never mind how. I do know, and now I'm in danger, too. Go to the police with that letter if you know where it is. Tell them about Sandi and send them out here to Brookham's estate. Please, Bev, this isn't a joke. They might do to me what they did to Deanie."

"They — Merky and his wife?"

"Maybe them," Julie whispered, forcing herself to say something, afraid of the possible truth. To admit that Tybalt could be involved was too much for her. She was still not sure, yet events seemed to cast a shadow over him. Deanie had been his girl, and Sandi, too!

"Sure. Say, be careful, kid. I hear that old place is a real chamber of horrors."

Julie agreed that she would try to be careful, then weakly replaced the receiver, hardly able to believe she had managed the call undetected. She had gambled her chances on Bev instead of the police, and she hoped she had made a wise move. If the police came here unprepared, they would be bowled over by Gerald's reputation, by Merky and Sarah. Bev knew something more. Hopefully her proof would reopen Deanie Jones's case.

The icy atmosphere of the stairs wafted around her as Julie wondered what to do. Pausing on the first landing, she debated whether to wait on the grounds for the police or to sneak back to her prison to lull Sarah

114

into thinking that nothing was wrong. Either way was a gamble. If only she could be sure of Tybalt. An idea seized her, one that made her skin prickle as she dwelled on it. She could gamble on Tybalt's innocence and place herself at his mercy, or at least she could appear to do so. That way, at least, she would know if he was involved in either Deanie's death or Sandi's disappearance. Perhaps he alone knew why the girls who visited Avon House were attacked after they returned to campus.

As Julie quietly trod the worn carpeting to the second landing she was thankful for Tybalt's casual joking mention of his room location, insinuating that she might like to know for future reference. At the time she thought it a typical male presumptuousness and had ignored his remark.

The door handle was cold beneath her grasp. Because it creaked, the door seemed to take hours to swing open, and Julie became conscious of a symphony of snores and whistles from the neighboring rooms.

Tybalt was sprawled half out of the covers. Moonlight shone from behind the clouds, washing the bed, suddenly bathing his dark muscular form in silver as the waving treetops changed the pattern of light. Julie closed the door, and leaned against it, her heart thundering a violent tattoo. Her emotion was partially stirred by the danger she was in, but also by her own vulnerability to Tybalt's attractiveness. Now he appeared as a romantic hero in a novel, and she was forced to shake herself free of the absurd vision of Prince Charming awaiting his true love, or whatever foolish notion the sight of him aroused. Standing beside the bed, Julie watched his chest moving rhythmically in sleep. For a moment she hesitated, reluctant to wake him, reluctant to destroy the comparative peace of the moment. Then she gripped his shoulder and shook him. "Tybalt, wake up."

He stirred and mumbled, reaching drowsily for the woman's hand he sensed, rather than felt, on his shoulder.

"Come on, wake up," she hissed, leaning over the bed. The next moment she found herself being pulled off balance, and she landed in a heap beside him on the blanket.

"Got you. Say, this is some surprise," Tybalt whispered hoarsely, carefully disentangling his bandaged arm from her weight, wincing at the pressure. "They told me you'd left. Guess you couldn't resist me after all. Came back, huh!"

Invitation to Danger

"For once will you stop being so sickeningly conceited!"

Taken aback by her angry words, Tybalt

blinked. Then he reached for the night lamp, and the room was bathed in light. "Well, at least someone fixed the lights. What do you want?"

"Not you. I just want some information."

"Look here, I can't believe this is really happening. You barge into my room, and when I make the natural conclusions, you fly at me. What information can I give you, besides the name of a competent psychiatrist?"

"I can imagine what Sarah told you. She was the one who locked me in the attic, the same place Deanie Jones stayed." Here he winced, and Julie plunged headlong into the rest of her speech. "I know that name makes you cringe, but I've got to know why. Something happened to that girl, and it wasn't suicide. The same thing could have happened to Sandi, and if I'm not careful it's going to happen to me. I feel I've a right to know what's going on, what the deep, dark secret is that everyone's trying to hide. And if you won't tell me what it is, I'll go to Gerald." Out of breath, Julie subsided.

The old bantering, playboy smile had left Tybalt's face, and his mouth had gone tight, the way it had been when he spoke of his mother's death at dinner last night. "Look, Julie, you probably think I'm lying, but I haven't the faintest idea what you're talking

117

about. In fact, I think Sarah's right when she says you're neurotic."

Seizing his wrists in frustrated anger, Julie shook him, tears starting in her eyes. "I'm not neurotic. Didn't you suspect anything when Nurse Sarah classed all your girl friends as neurotic? Didn't you suspect something fishy about Deanie's illness? She tried to blackmail Sarah, that's why she died. I think Sandi found out what she knew and was following up where Deanie left off. No slur against your masculine charm, incidentally, but that was the reason she was dating you."

Frustrated tears trickled down her cheeks as they stared at each other in silence. Julie's words had completely shocked Tybalt from his scoffing male assertiveness, leaving him a subdued stranger.

"There's no mystery connected with Sandi. We had a disagreement. If you want you can call her at home, or at Smith, or wherever she's hanging out licking her wounds, but don't accuse me of being involved in something illegal." He thrust back the bedcovers and leaped out of bed.

"I already called her, and she's supposed to be with you."

Tybalt paused, his clothes in his hand. There was no embarrassment between them, which for a moment Julie thought strange. To have been in his room a few days ago would have caused her concern, but the mixture of events that had happened since her arrival at Avon House seemed to have dulled her sensibilities. Now it seemed natural and right that she should be here, as if they belonged together. That was not true; after Sarah, Tybalt was a prime suspect, perhaps the only one.

"Now, I know that's a lie. There aren't any phones here."

"There's one."

"They were disconnected after Mother's death. It was Gerald's wish."

"It's in the kitchen. I called Bev, Sandi's roommate."

"And?"

"She said Sandi was supposed to be with you."

"Baloney. Sandi wrote me a note. Bev gave it to me herself."

Desperately Julie wanted to believe him. He was so convincing, his face suddenly honestly appealing. Why couldn't she believe him? After all, there was little evidence to the contrary. "Do you have the note?"

"Yes, I do — somewhere."

Her heart fell. Somewhere. What had she expected?

Tybalt was angry now, and he dragged his overcoat out of the closet. "You don't believe me, do you? Well, it's probably here in my pocket. I was wearing this when she gave me the note."

To her relief he produced a crumpled ball of paper and thrust it in her hands. Julie smoothed out the wrinkles and read it aloud. "You can forget this weekend. I've something more important to do. Perhaps Little Orphan Annie will go with you. Your *ex*-friend, Sandi."

Tybalt grinned sheepishly when she came to the Orphan Annie part. "Anne Orpha — the kids call her Orphan Annie. I guess Sandi was jealous. We went out together a few nights ago," he explained lamely. "So you see there was no big mystery to it, just a stupid temper flare-up."

"Did Bev know what the note said?"

He shrugged. "I guess not. I'm no fool. You don't think I let on it was a brushoff, do you?"

Julie could not help smiling. No, that was too much to expect of Tybalt; after all, he had a reputation to maintain. "Where is she, then?"

"I don't know. At home with her parents probably. They live in Dentonville."

"Does she have a car?"

"Yes. A foreign sports job. Bright green."

"With green-checked seat covers and big fringed cushions in the back?"

"Yes, something like that. Why?"

"That car's parked in the garages by the boathouse."

Tybalt's jaw dropped. "Are you sure?"

"Positive. I saw it yesterday, only then I didn't know there was any significance to it."

"Why would she follow me after turning down the invitation?"

"Maybe she didn't want you to know she was here."

"That's pretty dumb."

"She was Deanie's friend."

"You're kidding!"

"I know it seems strange because they were such opposites, but it's true."

Tybalt's expression had changed. Julie was not sure what the closed-off expression meant, but it made her wary. Had she revealed too much? "Sandi was probably puzzled over Deanie's suicide. Maybe she thought she'd learn something."

"So where's she hanging out? Don't tell me she's camping in her car," Tybalt snapped sarcastically.

"She wasn't there when I saw it. The gardener seemed to be in charge."

"What gardener?"

"Your grandfather's gardener. Oh, what was his name?" Julie searched her memory for the man's name. The incident had been so repelling, her mind seemed to have rejected his identity. "I know — Arthur something."

"It's news to me. Gerald uses some of the colony students in the spring and summer. They work to earn their keep, but as far as I know he lets things go in the winter. Are you sure he said he was a gardener?"

"Well, he didn't actually say. I just assumed so because he had a shovel and there was earth on his clothing." As she spoke, Julie's speech slowed. If Arthur the ghoul wasn't a gardener, what had he been digging? Surely he couldn't have been burying Sandi!

"Go ask him tomorrow who the car belongs to. Perhaps they just look alike. Maybe you've manufactured the whole mystery. This place has been known to make people weird."

"Weird enough to kill themselves?"

"I'd say so. The atmosphere's hardly conducive to sanity."

"So you think I'm merely following the pattern?"

"I didn't say that. Look, Julie, I'm as baffled as you are. I admit Sandi's actions appear odd, assuming that *is* her car in the garage. Then this guy Arthur — there's probably an explanation as to why he's in charge. Could be something Gerald forgot to mention."

Tybalt was giving logical explanations, but Julie did not want to accept them. Logic made little sense at Avon House, surrounded as they were by Shakespearean characters in a setting of gloomy decay. I know what I saw," she insisted stubbornly. "I know there's an attic room where Sarah locked me up. The only reason I'm here now is because I battered a window open and climbed onto the roof. Believe it or not, I've been nesting up there like some dumb bird since noon, thanks to a cup of Sarah's knockout coffee."

Tybalt frowned at her words. He began to speak, but Julie raced breathlessly on, desperate to finish her story. "And I know Deanie Jones used to be up there, too. Her suitcase was there beside the bed. Now, there's no sane explanation for all that."

"Agreed; it seems pretty crazy. Why don't we go downstairs and confront Sarah with the evidence? See what she says."

Julie was about to protest the inappropriate hour when she saw gray streaks of dawn already lightening the sky. It was Sunday. "She'll deny it."

"Sure, but if the room's rigged up like you say, we'll know she's lying."

"You can be sure it is," Julie insisted grimly, hearing the doubt behind his words.

She followed him into the chill, silent hallway, wondering if she was making a mistake. After all, if he was in league with Sarah in whatever scheme she had going, it wasn't likely he was going to admit it to her. She could have misplaced her trust.

"Come on, don't be scared." Tybalt's arm was warmly reassuring as they stopped before a closed door at the opposite end of the corridor. "This is Merky's room."

Tousled from sleep, Merky answered their knock, surprise registering on his pasty features as he saw them together. "It's early, isn't it, for social calls?" he muttered, tightening the cord of his dark robe. "What's wrong? The arm giving you trouble?"

In the jumbled excitement of the past few hours Julie had forgotten Tybalt's injury, and she was relieved when he shook his head in reply. "This is about something else. We'd like to talk to Sarah."

"Come in, then. Why it can't wait till a reasonable hour, I don't know," Merky grumbled, shuffling in down-at-the-heel slippers as he stood aside to let them in.

The bed was empty. Merky's surprise was genuine, Julie was sure of that. "She's not here. You mustn't be the only ones stirring before dawn."

As Julie and Tybalt descended the stairs Sarah appeared at the garden-room door, a long navy coat over her nightclothes, the edge of a lacy frill peeping from the hem of her coat.

"Sarah," Tybalt called.

Sarah leaped visibly at the unexpected voice. Her expression changed from shock to anger before assuming the practiced, enameled quality she usually affected. Julie was swift to note the registered emotions because she was looking for them. Tybalt remained unenlightened.

"Why, Julie, my dear, you've come back," Sarah exclaimed in feigned surprise.

"I never left. How well you know that."

"I've no idea what you're talking about."

"You know exactly what I mean. I've told Tybalt all about it. We want to see the attic room," Julie cried, throwing caution to the winds.

"The attic room? Which one in particular, dear?" Sarah asked innocently, coming to join them on the landing.

"The one where you locked me up. Don't worry, I can find it." Julie picked up her trailing, bedraggled skirts and scurried around the curving banisters to the next flight. Tybalt and Sarah followed, Sarah asking solicitously if his arm was painful, before adding her own reproaches about Gerald's unbalanced state of mind in encouraging such a spectacle to take place.

To her amazement, when Julie turned the doorknob, the door opened. The light revealed an empty room; the bed and the chest

125

were gone; even the dust was swept away. "You've cleaned it. Where's the bed?"

Sarah came to her side. "Come downstairs. Let me get you something to eat. The shock, you know, Tybalt, such a neurotic temperament —"

"I'm not neurotic," Julie cried, close to despair. "This is the room, you know that. Look, I'll prove it. There's the window I pried open. See!" In triumph she charged to the small porthole hanging lopsided in its frame.

"It's definitely been broken," Tybalt agreed, coming to her side.

"Yes, it has been broken. I must confess I did that when I tried to open it yesterday," Sarah explained, coming forward, a reproachful smile on her face. "The room was so stuffy. Really, Julie, you can do better than that."

All the fight left her as Tybalt exchanged significant glances with his aunt. He believed Sarah! Oh, how could he! She was lying, expertly perhaps, but they were still lies. "See, this is where I cut myself on the rusty hinge," Julie whispered in one last desperate attempt to be believed.

Sarah examined the gash on the limp hand pathetically thrust forward. "That is a bad cut. We'll put some antibiotic ointment on it before it gets infected. I don't suppose you're up to date on tetanus shots, either, are you?" Not waiting for an answer, Sarah took her by the elbow and pushed her ahead. "We'll get you a shot. Better to be safe."

"I don't want one," Julie protested, stumbling over the trailing skirts of her Juliet gown. "You can't make me have one."

"It's for your own protection. Tybalt will help, won't you, Tybalt?"

He shrugged. "I guess so, if you think she should have one. Come on, Julie, it's for you she's doing this," he added as they reached Sarah's room.

Manhandled, Julie found herself lying helplessly on Sarah's bed, the scratchy brocade cover beneath her face as they held her arm. She had no willpower to resist as she watched the needle descend, felt the jab, and saw Sarah's gleam of triumph. Then Tybalt patted her arm as with a grin toward his aunt he excused himself from the room.

So much for that! Julie thought, rubbing her arm where the puncture stung like fire. Weak light filled the room, glinting from a heavy sky. Everything was hopeless. Tears prickled her eyes as she burrowed deeper into the bed. She was alone, misunderstood, feeling drowsier and sadder as the drug took over. Merky came into the room, expressing surprise at her presence, his voice descending through muffled layers in her head. Then she was alone, drifting on a heavy cloud.

Chapter 8

When Julie awoke she thought she was in her own apartment. The strange, ostentatious Edwardian furnishings, penetrating fuzzily through her burning eyes, served to wake her abruptly, for there were no bobble-fringed curtains or five-foot vases overflowing with ferns at 112A North Elm. Where was she? Sitting up painfully and rubbing her eyes, which felt like sandpaper, Julie gradually remembered where she was and why. With a groan of dismay she fell back on the oversize pillow, resisting the temptation to slip back into oblivion. She must get out. Now, while Merky and Sarah were downstairs, believing her dead to the world for the rest of the day. Or was it night?

Slithering uncomfortably from the high bed, Julie padded to the window. It was so gloomy outside, it might already be night. To her surprise a flurry of white flakes swept past the window. The heavy cloud cover that had formed yesterday had left this early-season

129

snowfall. Great! Now it would be even more difficult to get away. Why hadn't she left last night when she had the chance? It must have been because of her stupid, ill-founded faith in Tybalt.

Clenching her fist, Julie turned from the cold-looking scene. At the moment she felt far from romantic about her former admirer; in fact, she was close to hating him for leading her into this situation, for pretending affection, and then just as quickly abandoning her to Sarah and her schemes. Still, perhaps he was as puzzled as she about the events surrounding Avon House; perhaps he thought the rest and the so-called tetanus shot were indeed for her own well-being. So much for Tybalt's powers of deduction.

Julie opened the deep mahogany wardrobe and looked for a coat. If she was going to escape in such bad weather, she would be a fool not to go prepared. Sarah's dark coat hung there, but when she took it out and put it on, it swept the floor in a majestic train. There were several dark overcoats; they must be Merky's. Julie put on Sarah's navy melton car coat, which fitted her full-length. There were a pair of knitted gloves and a woolen cap in the pocket, navy like the coat. The dark color would be conspicuous against a heavy blanket of snow, but in today's patchy sprinkling it would not matter.

Creeping into the cold hallway, Julie shuddered. These spooky, half-lit corridors always gave her the impression that someone watched from behind the closed doors. Hastily padding down the carpeting, Julie stuffed the skirts of her dress inside a cummerbund she fashioned from a torn piece of skirt. If she had more time, she could have changed her clothes or even worn something of Sarah's, yet this coat was repellent enough. She felt as if Sarah were attached to the clothing, for her Forest Flower perfume clung to the material, wafting in an unpleasant memory with every movement.

The swiftest way out was through the garden room. Though it seemed to be one of Sarah's haunts, Julie fervently hoped that right now Sarah was relaxing by the fireside. She stealthily edged between ferns and flowering tropical plants. Her journey negotiated safely, the swirling north wind whipped stinging flakes in her face as she stepped outside.

Almost hugging herself with relief, Julie broke into a run, following the path to the woods. A shiver passed over her, and she whipped about, fancying she felt someone's gaze on her back, but she saw no one. Hastening her steps, she thankfully disappeared into the camouflage of the undergrowth. Her thought was to head for the colony and get help. Surely they wouldn't be wacky like Gerald, for the actors at Cave Point were residents of the current world, not aging refugees from the past. They surely would help her find Sandi and establish her own credibility regarding Sarah's lies.

Somehow the thought of Sandi had propelled her, not toward the colony but toward the lake, for Julie saw the silent boathouses looming ahead. After a momentary pause she hit on an idea. If the car was in the garage, the key in the ignition as it had been the other day, her problems were over. She could drive to civilization.

Excitement spurred her forward. Julie peered through the grimy panes of the door to see the car still where it had been the day terrible Arthur offered to take her for a drive. Hopefully he was nowhere around, but unpleasant memories of his open, almost ghoulish admiration kept her wary. The main door was locked. To her relief she found an open side door.

Quietly closing the door, Julie blinked to accustom her eyes to the gloom; the garage overflowed with clutter, barely leaving room for the sports car. With shaking hands she dived toward the vehicle. The keys were gone. So intense had been her excitement, so sure her plan, that she almost succumbed to tears of disappointment.

Dropping onto a wooden crate, she rubbed her face with her hands and tried to think of an alternate plan. Something familiar caught her attention. Stacked on boxes by the door was the suitcase that had been upstairs. Hardly able to believe her good fortune, Julie leaped toward it and unsnapped the lock. Another disappointment was in store for her, for now the suitcase was empty. Only one thing kept her from wondering if she had imagined the whole thing. A luggage label still attached to the worn leather handle bore a name and address, barely discernible through a scuffed plastic window. The suitcase belonged to Deanie Jones, all right. Turning the tag around, Julie saw some writing on the reverse side, the letters written in pearlescent nail polish. The words were hard to decipher, for the letters had become thick where the polish had run. The message, seeming to come from beyond the grave, chilled her with shock. "Cave. Deanie J.," was what it appeared to say. For whom had Deanie written this message? Could it have been meant for Sandi? Had she read it and followed its instructions?

The more Julie worried about the dead girl's message, the more she was convinced that Sandi was in danger, or worse. If she had read those hastily scrawled words and investigated the cave, she could have met with foul play. Why else was her car here in this isolated garage? And the lost wallet with Sandi's driver's license had come from that cave. Though her stomach lurched with fear at the thought, Julie knew what she must do. She had to search the cave. And she must do it alone. Whatever was hidden there was comparatively safe as long as no one explored it.

Julie pulled off the luggage tag, then balled thick dust into crepey rolls with her sleeve to remove her handprints. No one else should see that message and follow her. Thrusting the tag into her coat pocket, she went outside, intent on her new purpose. Then she stopped abruptly, a gasp escaping her lips as she stared at a chasm before her in the earth, her shoes crumbling loose dirt at the brink. A chill shuddered through her, for this oblong trench looked like a grave. Was it for her? Or did it wait for Sandi Burns?

Fear and shock brought a cold sweat to her upper lip, sending it trickling down her arms and back inside the heavy warmth of the coat. Heart pounding, Julie carefully skirted the hole, already picturing her own white face lying bleakly beneath a thin blanket of fallen snow. The ground was not yet frozen; if they filled the grave and it snowed on top of it, no one would know it was there. This must have been what Arthur had been digging that day she had spoken to him, and she had not been aware of this sinister opening a few feet away.

Staying close to the walls of the building, Julie leaped back as a light was switched on in one of the rooms in the adjoining cottage. With a lurching stomach she recognized Sarah's angry, reproachful voice.

"I told you, no more secrets. Why couldn't you listen to me? Haven't I looked after you well? Heaven knows I've slaved to keep you at home. This is the thanks I get."

Julie strained to catch the words, wondering to whom she was speaking, yet not daring to look through the window in case her shadow alerted them to her presence. She did not have to wonder long, for the answer came amid clattering dishes. At first she did not recognize the voice; then when the noise stopped she knew who he was: Arthur, the shambling, leering handyman-cum-gardener-cum-gravedigger.

". . . Sarah, you know I don't mean it," he whined, pleading with her.

"It was bad enough before, trying to hush you up. It's too much."

"Don't be angry with Arthur. Sarah's always been Arthur's friend."

"Oh, shut up, you idiot — yes, idiot! Why I

didn't put you in a home instead of slaving to keep you, I'll never know. You've been nothing but trouble to me from the start. I can't go on. You'll have to turn yourself in and get help. There's nothing else for it."

"No!" A thunderous crash followed the screamed word.

Then Sarah spoke in softer, soothing tones, too low for Julie to hear. Her head reeling with her knowledge, Julie now knew he must be the brother Sarah told her she had supported by nursing. A flicker of pity came and went for Sarah, struggling to keep a retarded brother out of a home and in his own familiar environment. But what a foolish thing to do when he was demented enough to attack young girls, for surely that was what Sarah meant about hushing him up. Or was it? Her next words seemed to imply something else. And why, if she thought the attacker was Arthur, had she glared at Merky when they read of the attack in the morning paper?

"Come on, tell me where you put the pretty," Sarah coaxed, her tone wheedling and sugared.

"Won't tell you. Sarah's mean to Arthur. She won't let him drive the pretty car, either."

"It's for your own sake. I can't have you going off like the other night . . ."

"Bang! Bang! I love cowboys." Then he

136

laughed, bumping noisily about the room, shouting like an Indian.

Sarah was near the windows now. Julie could see her shadow on the curtain. Her head was in her hands, and it seemed as if she wept, for when she spoke, her voice wavered. "How I wish I could be sure that's all you did. If only you'd be honest with me. If you'd told me about this girl before, the one at the house needn't have been involved, I hate to have to do something to her, but there's no other way. Oh, Arthur, why didn't you tell me everything?"

"Didn't want to. Sarah's mean to Arthur. Won't let him go out. Won't let him see the pretty girls. Arthur wanted one for himself, that's all."

Julie was conscious of the beating of her heart deep within the double-breasted coat. What was he saying? Had he killed Sandi to keep her for himself? Was that why her car was in the garage? But one thing was clear. *She* was the girl at the house. And though Sarah "hated to do something to her," Julie knew that she would do whatever was necessary to protect her brother.

"Where's the girl? Please, Arthur, you've got to tell me, or I'll have to go to the police," Sarah threatened, her voice deep, almost masculine in its authority.

137

Through a chink in the curtain Julie could see Arthur now as he came to the window, and she pressed back against the wall, trying to remain out of sight. Thankfully she found his thoughts elsewhere, for he shook his head and smiled a peculiar smile. "I know, but I won't tell. Never. She's going to be mine."

"To think what I've gone through to have you ruin things for me now!"

The voices faded as Arthur clattered from the room, Sarah following. Julie slid down the masonry and huddled behind an evergreen to escape the howling wind swirling icily around the building. Could she be lucky enough to guess where Sandi was? Had Sandi gone to the cave as Deanie hoped, only to be followed by Arthur? She could be a prisoner there, or she could be the intended occupant of that grave between the garage and the house. Surely Arthur did not want to keep her for himself in that gruesome way!

Retracing her steps, Julie crossed behind the garage and headed for the cave, pulling the woolen hat close about her ears to keep out the numbing wind. She was afraid to explore the cave, and it might prove futile since she had no flashlight, but at least she could call out. If Sandi were still alive, she would answer her.

It was only a few minutes from the boathouse to the cave. Forcing herself to enter it, Julie soon was lost in the clammy, solid blackness of the rock chamber, her own footfalls echoing like the tramp of an army through the caverns and chambers of the network of underground rooms. Slowly she inched through the dark, feeling her way along the wet rock sides. From somewhere came the magnified drip of water, and she abruptly found its source as she went ankle-deep into an icy stream. Though on a hot day the caverns would feel uncomfortably cold, today the inner temperature was warmer than the snowy, blowing weather outside. She knelt and felt around on the rock to locate the width and depth of the stream, worried in case she had located the beginning of an underground river, for somewhere ahead she could hear a roaring that sounded like gallons of water crashing over rocks. She had no idea how deep these caves went, and she trembled at the thought of not coming out again. It had been foolish to enter without a light, without telling someone where she was. If something happened to her, no one would ever know.

Alarmed by the sobering thought, she crouched close to the water, grappling for a firm handhold on the eroded, slick rock. Something struck her fingers and she grasped it, wondering if she could be lucky enough to have found a book of matches. It was a book, but, disappointingly, too large for matches. Since it was too dark to investigate further, Julie put it in her pocket for later inspection. Then a sound came to her above the distant roaring, a scrabbling, echoing sound of footsteps. In panic she straightened up, banging her head on a rock projection. Clutching her injury, she moaned in pain. The flashing light she saw when she opened her eyes she at first attributed to the blow. It was a flashlight. Had Arthur come to claim his "pretty"?

"Julie, where are you? Are you anywhere inside?"

With a treacherous flood of relief she felt her knees weaken at the voice — Tybalt's. "Here I am, by the stream."

More scrabbling. Then the flashing red eyes of an animal startled her momentarily until she reocgnized Caesar's warm, moist tongue licking her face and neck. In a moment Tybalt joined him, illuminating her in a far-reaching yellow beam from a huge flashlight.

"Of all the idiots! Didn't I tell you not to explore?" he demanded in anger. "Are you all right?"

"Yes. I banged my head, but it's nothing serious."

He crouched beside her, his hands warm against the clammy iciness of her face. "You nut. You could be dead, you know. How on earth do you expect to explore without a light?"

Thankfully she laid her head against him, forgiving his seeming treachery for the moment, forgetting all but the relief of being rescued. "I found out a lot, Tybalt. This was only part of it."

"Is that so? You're supposed to be resting upstairs. When I saw you racing over the lawn, I figured this was where you were headed. Sarah would be hopping mad if she knew you were cave-exploring. Do you know it's twenty-eight degrees outside and snowing?"

"That won't matter when I tell you what I know. But first shine your light over here. Here's something I found in the cave."

Tybalt obeyed with a sigh of exasperation, clearly humoring her bizarre request. They examined the mysterious find. It was a small address book, the corners ragged from Caesar's ministrations. The paper, however, must have proved uninteresting, for he had abandoned it. Before she opened the first page, Julie's intuition told her the address book had belonged to Deanie Jones. Though she was prepared to see Deanie's name, she was not prepared for the shock she felt as she read, "Deanie Jones Brookham." What did that mean? Surely Deanie had not been a relative of Gerald Brookham!

"I don't understand."

"What's to understand? Come on. Let's go back." Tybalt straightened up. He caught her arm and shepherded her before him along the narrow trail, with Caesar leading the way, barking ringing, joyous greetings as he scrabbled along. With a curt word Tybalt quieted him.

"You're putting me off again. What do you know that you're not telling me?" Julie asked.

"Nothing."

"Don't tell me any more lies, Tybalt. I've been through too much already," Julie said determinedly. It was too late to sidestep the issues. There was something very strange going on here; already the puzzle pieces of Arthur and Sarah fitted in place. She must know what part Tybalt played.

"Sometimes lies can be for your own good," he snapped.

"I know Arthur is Sarah's retarded brother," she revealed unflinchingly. "I know something's happened to Sandi because Deanie confided a secret to her. Arthur could have murdered her. So you see, Tybalt, there's no time for half-truths."

"Okay, okay. I can see there's nothing for it but the whole story. You won't get off my back until you've wormed out the details."

His eyes flashed. "There were no secret trysts at the cave with either Deanie or Sandi, hard though that might be for you to believe. I just don't like caves, lady; they bother me. Okay?"

Attempting to regain her composure, Julie took several gulping breaths. She was afraid of him, but more afraid of what he was going to tell her. "If you'd been honest with me at first —"

"All right, supersleuth, but it isn't what you want to hear, far from it. I'm no murderer or campus maniac. You won't hear anything new about that, but I know what Deanie's tremendous secret was, her weapon to blackmail my grandfather. Gerald doesn't know, and if you tell him I'll wring your neck."

Tybalt's threat had meaning, and Julie backed away from him, the rock cold against her back. The cave was dark and she could not see his face, could only hear his voice rasping ping and hollow as it bounced back from the dripping walls.

"Deanie Jones was Gerald's daughter."

Julie's gasp echoed around the cavity, choking in her throat; of all the things she might have imagined, this was the furthest from her mind. "His daughter," she repeated.

"That's right. The outcome of a romance in his declining years with one of the cast members, I suppose. Anyway, Deanie thought she'd clean house with her secret. Gerald may have been a gay old dog once, but now he's a pillar of respectability — member of the Arts Council, local philanthropist, and patron of the theater. Merky and Sarah nearly had a cow."

"Why should the loss of respectability upset them so?"

"How should I know? Anyway, that's it, the only great dark secret I know. Come on, this place'll give me rheumatism. Trust me, you've got the whole bit."

Wary of his extended hand, Julie finally took hold of it, gripping the strength of his fingers as she leaped over the current. She tried to keep her distance from him, but somehow she failed, and she was glad. The warmth and comfort of his presence were too much for her. Tears prickled behind her eyes, and she shook her head to clear them. "Thanks."

"Don't mention it."

"I wish you'd told me sooner."

"Why? So you could laugh your head off at me for romancing my aunt?"

"No, so that I wouldn't have spent all this time thinking you'd had a hand in some terrible crime."

Tybalt snorted at her words, drawing her

toward the distant beam of light. Out in the daylight her fears began to evaporate. Already her mind returned to the puzzle she had unearthed. Tybalt's explanation might cover a couple of things, but not what had actually happened to Deanie, or what might have happened to Sandi.

"Do you suppose they were angry because she might share in Gerald's estate?" she asked.

Tybalt stopped on the path, his face growing serious. "I never thought about that angle. You could have something there."

"Did they have Arthur kill her?"

"No. She overdosed. The police verified that. Besides, what makes you so sure this Arthur really is Sarah's brother? You told me he was a gardener."

"I eavesdropped on their conversation."

"Good Lord, is he living in the house, too?"

"No, in that cottage by the boathouse. Didn't you know about him?"

"Sarah said she had a brother who wasn't all there, but I didn't know he was staying here. What makes you think he killed anybody? Despite his crazy romantic ideas concerning you, he could be harmless, you know."

Julie fiercely shook her head. She felt angry again because once more he was dismissing her discovery as insignificant. "Look, I overheard her telling him off about taking the car to town. Then she wanted to know what he did to Sandi. Where she was. And if that isn't convincing enough, Deanie Jones's suitcase is in the garage." Surprised by the anguished look that crossed his face, Julie stopped. "Why can't you bear to talk about her?"

"It's not that I can't bear to talk about her, it's guilt. Don't look surprised. I'm human after all. If I'd never brought her here, she might still be alive. That's the reason I hate to drag her name into every conversation."

"Are you sure you've told me everything?"

"Listen, Julie, sweetheart," Tybalt pleaded, taking her hands. "They were fun; they meant nothing to me. Whatever went on, murder was definitely not part of it."

"I want to believe you."

"Then do it. You mean too much for me to want the same to happen to you. Besides, I have my own suspicions about the campus attacker. Merky."

"Merky!"

"He's always had an eye for young girls, and weird as he is, I wouldn't put anything past him. You know how he can submerge himself in another character, and you saw the way Sarah practically accused him when we read that newspaper article. Even if today she's blaming Arthur, there was something behind that display the other morning. If anyone has a right to prejudge him, it's her."

The theory was sound. Merky's chameleon-like characteristic was immediately suspect. Did he have a hidden personality that aped some fictional murderer with whom he identified? "The idea's not bad, but it still doesn't explain Arthur's driving into town or Sarah's hushing something up."

They were in sight of the house, and Caesar bounded ahead to scratch at the garden-room door.

"Forget it, Julie. Deanie committed suicide, and my mother and father committed suicide. This house gives people the creeps, that's all. There's no murderer lurking about."

"Did your mother commit suicide for some reason I don't know?" she ventured, knowing the subject was a delicate one.

"There was an illness in Grandmother Brookham's family — it has no real bearing on your detective work, but seeing that I'm making a clean sweep, I might as well tell you this, too." Tybalt's face was tight and grave. He stopped at the garden-room door and began to brush snowflakes from the heavy growth of ivy about the door. He didn't look at her. "We've an inherited muscular disease — Graves' syndrome, Green's syndrome —

anyway, Grandmother had it, and Mother developed it in her thirties. That's why she needed a nurse. It's a progressive ailment that eventually makes you bedridden."

"You're pretty nonchalant about it," Julie said, feeling as if she had been struck in the face. Was this the reason why Tybalt lived so recklessly?

"That, my sweet, comes from being born a male; the disease passes only to the females. Maybe that's why she ended things — or it could have been from Nurse Sarah's cheering commentary on the charms of total helplessness. Ready to go in?"

Chapter 9

The house seemed deserted. A perking coffee-maker greeted them cheerily in the dining room, where the table was set with appetizers and cutlery.

"Guess Merky's driven into town," Tybalt commented, seizing a handful of canapés before retiring to the hearth.

Julie hoped Sarah was still at her brother's cottage.

"Still want to go home, several days late though it may be?" Tybalt asked with a grin, stretching his legs to the blaze.

"I don't know. You still haven't convinced me that I'm going out of my skull," Julie said, joining him beside the fire.

"I don't think the person's born who could do that."

His smile was lazy, his eyes lambent in the fire's glow. Julie was forced to rouse herself, for it would be so easy to escape into the promised thrill of his embrace and forget the silly mystery of Deanie and Sandi. Silly mystery — now *that* was a bit of Tybalt's brain-washing if ever there was one. She stood, unbuttoning the borrowed coat.

"Guess I'll return these things before the owner misses them."

"Okay. When you've changed, come on down. I'll be here."

His husky promise still ringing in her ears, Julie walked down the corridor, but away from the stairs and toward the garden door. If Tybalt took her home to Smith, she would never know what had really happened; she would never have a chance to show Sarah up for what she was.

Almost laughing in disbelief at her own foolhardiness, Julie retraced her steps to the cave, Tybalt's large flashlight gripped in her hands. If Sandi were hidden there, Julie was determined to find her, providing she wasn't miles deep in the caverns. Tybalt said he had not rendezvoused here with Sandi, yet her billfold had come out of the cave, borne triumphantly in the gooey mouth of the Labrador. Which meant that even if she was not here now, she had been at one time. She could be imprisoned here with only Arthur knowing it, secretly hidden away for his own amusement — or she could be dead.

Bolstering her courage, Julie plunged forward inside the cave, raking the slick walls and ceiling with the flashlight's beam in the hope of finding some sign of habitation. If she had had more foresight, she would have brought Caesar so that he could retrace his steps to the old haunt from where his treasure had emerged.

The underground river was getting closer. Julie could hear the splattering, booming echo as it foamed down the rocks. Suddenly, as she rounded a bend, the river tumbled white before her, sudsily outlined in the yellow disc of light. She could go no farther. Surely this journey was not going to end as futilely as the last one. A small rock bumped against her leg and she caught her breath, wondering for one terrifying moment if a rock slide would seal her forever in the secret confines of Cave Point.

Another rock followed, then another. Weak with fright, Julie looked upward, shining her beam toward the source, and gasped in shock as she saw a trussed-up bundle on a ledge about six feet above the ground. With a gulp of relief she realized that the bundle was bouncing on its shelf, frantically trying to signal her with the falling rocks.

Warily Julie found a foothold and climbed upward. She shone her flashlight on the face of the mummylike body, then gasped, "Sandi!" The girl's mouth was bound by a colored handkerchief, and with numb, shaking fingers Julie loosened the knot and slipped the gag off.

"Thank God for that!" Sandi croaked, trying to roll off the ledge.

Julie helped her to the floor of the cave and then struggled with the knotted cords about Sandi's legs and hands. At last Sandi could worm herself free, and she let out a tremendous sigh of relief.

"Wow! I don't know who you are, girl, but you're as welcome as —"

"Julie Brown. From Merky's drama group."

Sandi moved the pool of light forward, guiding Julie's arm until she had illuminated her face. "Oh, hi, I know you, don't I? What on earth are you doing here?"

"That's a long story. I came with Tybalt and got all involved in this mess. How long have you been here?"

"A few days. It's hard to tell in a cave. God, there are bats in here, girl. Scads of them. I think I've lost a few years' growth." Sandi was trying to make herself heard above the cascading water.

"Who put you here, Sarah?" Julie asked, motioning Sandi ahead on the narrow, low-roofed walkway.

"Merky's old lady? No. It was some crazy caretaker. Wow! Is he weird! Says he's keeping me for his pretty. His sister won't let him have a pretty, or something like that. I really thought I'd had it."

"Did he hurt you?" Julie faltered, not really knowing how to phrase her question, but hoping Sandi understood.

"Heck, no, which was a relief at least. He just wants to look at me. He came in and brought food. Told me it was no use to shout down here. After virtually losing my voice, I realized he was right. After all, who goes poking in caves?"

"Me."

Sandi smiled and gripped Julie's arm. "Thanks. You've saved my life."

"What I want to know is what Deanie Jones told you. That's why you're here, isn't it?"

Sandi paused in the act of discarding the ropes. "What do you know about that?"

"That Deanie was Gerald's daughter and she was going to blackmail him. Sarah found out and disposed of her."

Sandi hesitated, stamping her feet to restore the circulation. "Well, I guess if you know that much, I'd better clue you in on the rest."

"Come on, keep moving. Talk as we go. At least we don't have to scream our heads off now. This place is giving me the creeps," Julie said impatiently, motioning Sandi ahead.

"Why, it's almost like home," Sandi quipped as she edged along the path. "That crazy dog should've brought you the message I gave him. Dumb animal."

"You gave him a note?"

"Not exactly. At first Weirdo didn't tie my hands. I threw that dog my billfold, hoping he would take it to someone and get me rescued. I didn't have any paper or pencil."

Julie smiled a bit guiltily. "Well, he did that, all right. He gave it to me. But at the time I thought it was merely an overlooked memento of one of Tybalt's romantic interludes."

Sandi snorted, quickening her steps as light filtered in from outside. A blast of cold air greeted them from the crisp, white world, and Julie grinned. "I forgot to tell you it snowed."

"Great."

It was coming down heavier now. On her journey to the cave the snowstorm had stopped, but now Julie's tracks were being covered over. "Your car's in the garage over there. I don't suppose you have a key on you?"

Sandi shook her head. They crawled to a vantage point on the rocky crag and crouched under the overhang to map out their plans. The gray world below seemed hopelessly lonely, and Julie shivered at the bleak scene of bare trees and iron-gray water slowly dissolving in a fluttering white veil.

"Tell you what I do have, though, a bundle of letters from Gerald Brookham to Deanie's mother, plus a copy of Deanie's birth certificate. She hid them in a box in the cave after she'd mailed a letter to me telling me where to look. I have it at school. Deanie was sure Merky's old lady murdered Tybalt's mother with an overdose of pain killer so there'd be one less person in the running for Avon House. She was her nurse, you know. Besides that, she supplied Deanie with some drugs — just long enough to get her guard down — then she turned against her. Deanie said she wasn't the only one getting drugs from her. Sarah made her stay at the house by holding out on the stuff. She stayed in the attic so no one would know she was there. Sarah didn't know Deanie had already stashed her insurance in the cave."

"Are you sure? About the drugs, too?" Julie gasped.

"Well, I've only got what Deanie told me to go on. She didn't leave much proof. After all, what real proof can you have? Deanie was a strange kid, but she was all right. I believed her. She had a real struggle to make ends meet. I guess she thought Gerald and his millions could help her on her way. That was pretty mercenary, but I can't blame her; she had some pretty good aces up her sleeve."

"Why did she commit suicide? Or did Sarah fake that?"

"I wish. Unfortunately Sarah was safely visiting in Hartford at the time of Deanie's death. If she'd been around Smith, we could have neatened things up. Deanie probably overdosed; she was pretty strung out on drugs by then. She told me she hadn't long to live, so she might as well enjoy herself before she kicked off."

"You mean she thought Sarah was going to kill her?"

"No, not that. It was something out of Sarah's control."

"What?"

"They've some terrible hereditary illness in the Brookham family. Deanie was petrified when she found out. It's a muscular disorder that leaves you helpless. Tybalt's mother had it; that's why she needed Sarah." Sandi's voice cracked, husky from its disuse.

"Yes, Tybalt told me about her. Gerald's wife had it, too. Graves' syndrome, or whatever. Right?"

"Yeah, it sounds right," Sandi agreed, rubbing her legs.

"It's inherited through the female side of the family. Gerald doesn't have it; Merky and Tybalt are both okay. It came from their grandmother's family."

Sandi was puzzled, finding Julie's statement irrelevant. "So what? Where does that leave Deanie?"

"It means she couldn't have the illness, even though Gerald was her father. She wasn't related to the female side of the family."

"Hey, you're right." Sandi's face broke into a grin. "Smart thinking. Even imagining something like that's going to happen to you is enough to scare anyone to death."

"Especially if someone wanted you to think you already showed the symptoms. While she lived, Deanie was an heir to Gerald's estate," Julie declared in a rush of triumph.

"And who knows more about things medical than Sarah? What a diabolical idea! Deanie said Sarah killed Tybalt's mother, so I thought she'd actually bumped her off; but now you bring this point up, I see there's more than one way to get rid of someone. If you can talk them into doing the job themselves, you get off scot-free. Right?"

Julie nodded. Sarah could be very convincing. After the contradictory episodes that had taken place this weekend, Julie had more than once found herself wondering about the state of her own sanity. "Sarah wants this house so badly. Surely Merky will inherit part of the estate; he's Brookham's son. Taking such risks seems unnecessarily foolish."

"Oh, I don't know. Maybe she thinks Merky will dump her for someone at the college.

Then she'd be out of the running for good."

"Merky fools around to that extent?" Julie gasped, hunching deep in her coat as a gust of wind sought her out, swirling snow against her face.

"Sure. Don't tell me old Lothario hasn't made a pass."

"Not yet."

Sandi laughed. "He will. He must be problem enough for Sarah without long-lost relatives popping up."

Sandi's joking statement brought Tybalt's theory to mind. Could he be right about Merky's involvement in the series of campus attacks? "Have you been to Avon House before?"

"Once. Tybalt usually gets around to bringing his girl friends here. Why?"

"Were you attacked?"

Sandi paled, her mouth going dry, and she licked her lips. "How did you know? I never told anyone."

Julie stared at her in shock. "I didn't know. It's just that Tybalt told me all the girls who'd been attacked had been here first. I wonder if it's Arthur — the Weirdo, as you call him. He's Sarah's brother."

"Wow! What an anchor — Merky and the Weirdo. Poor woman. I almost feel sorry for her. I kept quiet about being attacked. I wasn't really hurt. Nothing's happened since."

"Did Merky make passes at the other girls involved? I'm sure they were all good-looking. Tybalt doesn't seem to go for slouches."

"I know he made a play for Deanie. She really got wild with him before he'd take no for an answer. The others were probably in the same boat. You don't suspect Tybalt of attacking them out of jealousy over Merky, do you?"

"No. Why should Tybalt attack them? They were already his," Julie dismissed this pointedly while Sandi nodded in agreement. "Merky's more likely to have done it in anger because he was rejected."

"Wow! Have I just remembered something! There's a key in one of those magnetic holders under the bumper. If we can get in the garage, we can make a break for it."

"You go. I'll stay here. I want to talk to Tybalt again and give Merky a chance to make a play for me."

They scrambled to their feet, and Sandi put her arm loosely around Julie's shoulder. "Are you that brave or just nuts?"

"A little of both, I think."

The garage was dark, the side door still unlocked. Trembling as she led the way, Julie took Sandi inside, carefully closing the door. If they could start the car and open the door

— but she wasn't going to leave. The reminder was a jolt. It would be so easy to join Sandi in the car, to disappear into the world of snowy trees and safety. But she couldn't go yet. The attacks would go on, and she couldn't live with all those unanswered questions. The smattering of knowledge would haunt her every time she read about another female victim. She would always wonder if it was Arthur, or Merky . . . or even Tybalt.

"Here it is."

With a pitching stomach Julie kept a lookout while Sandi fitted the key in the ignition. "You'd better open the door, dope," she snapped tensely.

"I thought you'd do that for me," Sandi replied with a sheepish grin.

Julie opened the protesting mechanism, trying in vain to do it quietly. The groaning hinge seemed to echo throughout the countryside, and she listened for sounds of pursuit from the adjoining cottage. A light still shone from an upstairs window, but no one came out to investigate.

"I think we made it. Sure wish you'd reconsider and come with me," Sandi whispered in a final bid. "When this thing pulls out of here, you'd better be flying, because they're going to be here in a flash."

"I know. Go to the police and show them

the letter. They mightn't believe things as we see them, but they'll investigate. Tybalt's more or less on my side, and I don't think Sarah will do anything yet. Sandi, will you call my mom? She's listed in the directory — Mrs. Jordan. Tell her I'm okay; she might worry if she can't reach me."

"Sure. 'Bye and good luck. We'll laugh about this when we get back — I hope."

Sandi fired the ignition on and the car died. She tried again. On the third attempt it took hold, and the green sports car shot out of the garage, spun completely around on the icy ground, then, righting itself, headed for the road.

To her horror Julie found that the sound of the grinding ignition and the roar of the engine had brought the enemy to life. With a cry of dismay she plunged toward the undergrowth as the back door opened and Sarah, dressed in a man's overcoat, ran outside. Arthur, pulling a cap on his head, followed her. They raced inside the empty garage, Sarah shouting and fuming, Arthur looking bewildered. Julie decided it would be foolish to wait here on their doorstep. She would run for it; the snow was still coming down, and it might cover her tracks.

She had almost reached the bend in the road, a few yards from Cave Point, when she heard Sarah's bellow of rage, and she knew she had been spotted. Fright choked in her throat as she tried to run faster on legs pliant as rubber. Two figures ran past the garage. Sparing a moment to look back, she was surprised to see that they weren't pursuing her, disappearing instead inside the house, only to reappear a few minutes later. Maybe they had called for assistance. The thought made her move faster, deep into the woodlands, afraid to veer from the path because of the treacherous undergrowth masked by soft, drifting snow. The flakes were dwindling now, and in alarm Julie realized that all they had to do was to follow her tracks. Her footprints would lead them to her. She could not even brush out the tracks with a branch like the Indians did, for this white unmarred road would show any mark of human passage. The only thing to do was to hide in the bushes until the afternoon light had gone.

Through a break in the clouds the sun shone a brilliant orange for a moment before it slid down the hillside behind the trees. Soon it would be dark and they would not be able to follow her tracks; then she would try to make it back to the house. Surely they would not kill her just to fill that waiting grave. They might not even know which girl had left in the car, but then, since Sarah must be desperate by now, whoever occupied that sinister black hole would make little difference.

Two running figures emerged on the path, then veered off on side journeys into where the brush was thin. Hopefully Arthur would be little help, but Sarah was a formidable force to reckon with. Julie crouched beneath the vast, dense branches of a huge magnolia, burrowing deep in the soft earth cover of fallen leaves and decay. She dared not move now; they were too close.

"I've gone through too much. You won't get away," Sarah cried, crashing through the undergrowth, making no attempt to be quiet. Her passage was akin to an enraged rhino, and Julie shuddered as the minutes ticked by. The white path was marred by the prints of Sarah's black orthopedic shoes showing in stark relief on the snow.

Out of breath, her voice wavering with mingled rage and fatigue, Sarah shouted, "Come out! It's no use hiding from me. The dog will be here in a minute."

Julie digested the startling news; they must have called Merky for help. Sarah did not know Julie had little fear of Caesar, but in a few moments her hiding place would be discovered. For, never missing a chance to play, once he picked up her scent, the Labrador would make a beeline for her leafy shelter.

The wind moaned eerily through the pines, sighing like a voice in the treetops, drowning Sarah's angry muttering as she resumed her search. Grief throbbed in Julie's throat, choking her breath. If only she had trusted Tybalt and told him what she intended to do, she could at least hope for rescue from him. As it was, she was at Sarah's mercy. In a few minutes two hostile forces would join against her, ably assisted by her friendly hiking companion, Caesar.

The last fiery rays of the sun were extinguished as the hillside plunged into darkness. A rosy tinge lingered a moment on the white ground on the west slope of the hill, fading from purple to black as she watched.

"All right, you fool, if it takes all night I'll find you."

Sarah's voice came closer, and Julie mouthed a silent prayer of thanks for her dark clothing. Then something she had not given any thought to betrayed her hiding place: pollen from the lush fall undergrowth made her nose tickle. She held her breath, desperately trying not to sneeze as she squeezed her nose in her fingers, for Sarah's dark shadow was only a few feet away. The sneeze was finally subdued into a sputtering cough, not loud, but loud enough for Sarah's sharp ears to catch it.

Sarah whirled in a flurry of anger. "Come out of there!"

Large hands reached out and grabbed at her. For a wild moment Julie thought of scrabbling through the brush in an effort to escape, but she decided against it. Sarah hauled her from beneath the overhanging branches as easily as if she had been a rag doll. In a moment Arthur was at her side, his vacant face looming through the grayness. "Which one?" he asked.

"Julie Brown, the imposter."

"I'm not an imposter. It's not my fault you were so suspicious you picked the wrong girl."

"Right. Not your fault, sweetie, but your bad luck," Sarah snapped unpleasantly, thrusting Julie before her and bending her arm behind her back in Sarah's famous wrestling hold.

Arthur trudged behind them, nonchalantly humming to himself. Crying from the pain, Julie stumbled on through the dark, not expecting, and not getting, any mercy from Sarah. This viselike grip must be the one she had perfected on uncooperative patients during her tenure as private nurse. The small lighted cottage came into view through the gloom, and Julie was thrust inside the cluttered living room.

"Get on the phone to the house. Tell Merky to call it off. Now, can I trust you to do it right?" Sarah snarled at Arthur, who had drifted toward the table where a large, half-finished jigsaw puzzle was spread out. "You can play later."

While Sarah's attention was distracted, Julie took advantage of her slackened grip and darted for the door. She reached the handle, the exciting smell of freedom in her nostrils as she wrenched the door ajar. That was as far as she got. Sarah bellowed in anger and grabbed her, delivering a thumping, jarring blow to her head. Julie saw the cluttered room whirl crazily in brilliant flashes of light.

"Why couldn't you leave us alone? It's too late now. I can't let you go — you have to understand that. If it hadn't been for Tybalt, I might even have liked you."

Julie barely comprehended the monotonous voice, its meaning horribly vague until she recognized Sarah and Arthur leaning over her. She was choking with a wad of material crammed in her mouth.

"Pretty, pretty." Arthur leered down at her, his rough hands stroking her cheek. Julie shuddered.

"Stop it. Leave her alone. If it weren't for you, we might not have to do this," Sarah cried, pushing him aside. "If you'd told me about the girl instead of trying to keep it a secret. If you hadn't hidden the car."

Arthur whimpered like a child, rubbing his eyes as if he would cry, his slack mouth pouting in disappointment. "Pretty car, that's what I wanted. You never let me have one. Never," he muttered in defense.

Sarah sighed. "Yes, pretty, that's all you think about."

Arthur shambled away and began to clatter dishes on the table. Julie rubbed her head against her drawn-up knees.

Watching her action, her captor grinned ruefully. "I'll get you an aspirin for your headache if you like."

Julie vigorously shook her head, gritting her teeth against the pain. By now any medication administered by Nurse Sarah was suspect; probably a massive dose of knockout pills.

"Okay, suit yourself. Don't say I didn't offer."

A phone rang in another room and Sarah went to answer it, her efficient voice easily discernible through the thin walls. With a sinking heart Julie knew who that call was from. As she had feared, the police were not convinced by Sandi's excited story of imprisonment at Avon House.

"Such terrible lies. Why, I can't believe it! Now, I ask you, Officer, can you credit someone's being imprisoned in an attic at Avon House? What . . . two girls? Oh, really. Now, would Mr. Brookham allow such things to go on? These girls — too much to drink, too many late night movies. . . . Yes, of course, if we need you we won't hesitate to call. Good evening."

Sarah stormed back into the living room, her dark eyes flashing in anger at her brother, who was aimlessly fitting together the jigsaw puzzle. "Didn't I tell you to have them shut the gates when we heard the car? When I left you to call, I thought it was the least you could do —" She broke off her reproaches, finding Julie's gaze on her. "Well, your friend went to the police at Winton with some cock-and-bull story about Deanie and yourself being my prisoners. If the gates had been closed, we could have avoided the embarrassment. Still, it doesn't matter. No one believes her, anyway. Sorry."

Julie gasped in relief as Sarah loosened the tea-towel gag in her mouth. "They have to believe her. It's true," she blurted as soon as she was able.

"You're pretty naïve. Just because something's true, it doesn't mean anyone believes it. In this case, the word of Merky and Gerald Brookham overruled a hysterical girl's lies. Simple, isn't it? They only relayed the call to me from the house to add more weight, seeing as I'm typecast as the villain by your bouncy little friend."

"I thought Gerald didn't know about the phone in the kitchen."

Sarah smiled maliciously. "He doesn't, my dear. Merky does a marvelous imitation of the old goat."

Throughout the exchange Arthur stolidly worked his puzzle, frowning over the difficult scene of snow-capped mountains and purple-tinged lakes. "She'll be my pretty now," he said, treating Julie to one of his hideous admiring smiles.

"No," she gasped, shuddering as he wandered from his puzzle to pat her hair, his fingers stroking the silken strands admiringly until Sarah thrust him aside.

"Get back to your toys. This girl isn't going to stay here to be your *pretty,* or anything else. She can make a whole lot of trouble for me — you, too, so you'd better get used to the idea."

Arthur scowled and went back to the table, but his interest in the jigsaw puzzle was lost. Sarah walked back to the kitchen, and she and Arthur were alone for the first time since she had been brought to the cottage. Helplessly she looked about the room, searching for a means of escape, but she could find none. Beyond the windows a thin white blanket stretched as far as she could see, the light from the windows casting elongated golden shapes over the snow.

"Sorry Sarah's so mean," Arthur apologized, treating her to a childish grin. "Don't like her any more now; never like her again."

His declaration was surprising, and his reversal of loyalties sparked a faint hope of cooperation. "Will you let me go, Arthur?" Julie whispered hoarsely, glancing toward the kitchen from where the smell of frying bacon wafted. She heard Sarah whistling tunelessly as she cooked.

"Can't do that. Sarah'd be angry."

"You said she was mean to you. Wouldn't you like to go somewhere that everyone's nice to you? Not mean like Sarah."

Emphatically Arthur shook his head. "Sarah's my mother."

"No, she's your sister," Julie corrected with a sinking heart, her hopes of escape dwindling by the minute.

"Yes, that's right. Mother and Father died a long time ago. Are your mother and father dead?"

Julie shook her head, numbness gripping her body. How ironic it was to think that if she had been able to get along with Pete Jordan, this unbelievably horrible weekend would never have taken place; she would have been safely at home. A tear slid down her cheek to splash on her hand.

"Don't cry. You miss your mother and father, don't you?" Arthur asked with genuine concern. Touchingly he produced a clean handkerchief and held it out to her. "Here."

His innocent gesture brought more tears, and Julie felt her heart wrenched with pity for him, for her situation, for the utter hopelessness of everything. If she could just lie back and go to sleep and forget everything . . .

"Do you two want to eat?" Sarah rapped from the doorway.

Arthur bounded toward the kitchen, his pity for Julie dissolved before the thought of a plate of bacon and eggs for supper. Alone in the darkened room, Julie looked away from the small lamp on the table. The light made her eyes dance with strange black shapes. She was so tired, so weary. . . .

"Here, you, this is a waste of good food, but I'm a soft touch." Sarah thrust a plate of hot food before her, and Julie's mouth watered at the appetizing smell. The last thing she had eaten was an olive canapé when she returned from her preliminary cave exploration with Tybalt all those centuries ago.

"There's no use going soft in the head. We've got to get rid of her. There'll just be the two of us soon, Arthur. You'll see, it'll all be worth it." Sarah's soothing words drifted from the kitchen. Her voice glowed with kindness, and Julie wondered if she was being sincere, or if she was only using Arthur until her goals were achieved. A few more minutes alone with him, and Julie might have been able to talk him into freeing her.

Chapter 10

Events progressed logically, almost like a bad play that she had watched before, as Arthur and Sarah came back into the room, still dressed in outdoor clothing.

"Now, it's up to you, Arthur. You must do it — you understand, don't you? If you're not very careful, they might come to take you away; then you wouldn't see me any more."

Arthur listened attentively, all traces of his former sympathy for Julie evaporated. In dismay Julie gazed at his set face, wondering how Sarah could have won him so easily to her side with such simple bait as bacon and eggs. But won him she had. Without changing his expression, he came to Julie and pulled her up by her wrist. For all his childishness, he was surprisingly strong.

"Please, Arthur, don't listen to her," Julie pleaded desperately.

"You shut up and do what you're told!" Sarah cried. Then, motioning to Arthur, she urged, "Go on, get on with it."

Arthur grabbed Julie's arms and propelled her to the door. Her first impulse was to fight for freedom, but thinking that she still might have a chance to sway him to her side, she decided not to resist. When he could see that she was not going to cause trouble, Arthur slackened his grip.

The cold night was bright with moonlight now. The sky had cleared, and soft light sparkled over the crisp snow, etching tall black tree shadows in silver. Arthur paused outside the door, his mouth hanging agape at the scene.

"Pretty, isn't it, Arthur?" Julie whispered, taking advantage of this curious facet of his nature.

"Pretty," he agreed.

"We could walk in it if you like."

Clearly he was tempted, for his thoughts were registered on his face as he stood beneath the yellow porch light, his expression a curious mixture of that of a greedy child, and something else: it was the something else that frightened Julie.

"Can't," he said, shaking his head, but he did not move.

"Sarah won't know."

Her coaxing made him waver, for his face broke into the eager, childlike look of pleasure that she had seen before. "We won't tell Sarah."

"Of course not."

"We could go to the lake."

"If you'd like." Her heart was thundering with fright as she wondered if she could manage to escape, or to talk him into going to either the colony or the house. It would be so simple. But even as she thought it, she heard Sarah's voice on the telephone, her words filtering through the silence. Sarah was near the window in the kitchen, her shadow dark above the yellow cafe curtains, her back to them, already convinced that the problem of disposing of their captive was on the way to being solved.

"This is Mrs. Brookham — we spoke earlier. There's something I'd like to tell you. For months I've shielded someone. I can't go on like this —"

Was that Sarah breaking into tears? They sounded so fake, so melodramatic, yet the police did not know Sarah as Julie did. Appalled, Julie looked at Arthur, who had heard the conversation but attached no significance to it. "She's going to turn you over to the police, Arthur."

"Sarah?"

"Yes, listen; she's calling them now. Let me go. Then there's nothing they can do to you."

From inside came the sound of heroic sniffles as Sarah plowed on with her dialogue. "It has to do with those shocking attacks on Smith's campus. At first I wasn't sure, but now I know who's responsible. I must tell someone."

"What does she mean? I've never been to Smith. Sarah won't let me go. She's afraid someone will see me," Arthur grumbled indignantly, stepping into the crunchy snow.

"You mean you've never been there? Are you sure?"

He shook his head emphatically. "Never."

Who could be responsible, then? Was Sarah going to put the blame on her brother in the hope he would escape prosecution because of his mental state? That left Merky as the real suspect — or Tybalt.

"Come on. Arthur doesn't want to listen any more."

His face was determined as he pulled Julie's arm, propelling her down the path to the lake. At least they weren't going to the garages to use the grave; that was one thing in her favor. Ahead, through the trees, a light flashed. Arthur pulled her into the shelter of a thicket of shrubs. Who could be out there? Julie prayed harder than she ever remembered praying before, knowing that her life hung on the slim balance of this man's intelligence.

"Who is it?" he gasped, his voice quaking. "Did Sarah send the police for me?" His arm trembled against her. "Did she?"

"It's too soon for them. Perhaps it's someone coming to help you," Julie soothed, wondering how she could feel the least bit of sympathy for her would-be assassin, let alone bother to reassure him. She must be nuts.

"Yes, Arthur needs someone to help him."

Julie patted his arm, barely containing her racing excitement, knowing that as long as he was afraid of Sarah and the police, freedom lay only moments away. "Come on, let's find out who it is," she decided bravely.

As they stepped onto the path a suddenly charging black flurry collided with her legs, and she fell backward, stunned by Caesar's boisterous greeting.

"Thank goodness you found her," a voice said in the darkness. "I could have been in these damned woods all night."

Julie quailed in horror at the voice. It was Merky's.

"Sarah's on the telephone," Arthur supplied with returning confidence.

"Yes. Good. Hey, it's the quiet one. Good evening, Miss Brown. I'm sorry to meet you in circumstances like this," Merky said, pushing down the eager dog. "You never liked me very well, did you? That's a pity. If you had liked Tybalt even less, maybe you wouldn't have to end so tragically."

"Look, Sarah's on the phone to the police, turning in whoever attacked those girls on campus."

Merky nodded. "Yes, she said she would."

"She's accusing Arthur, and it's not him, is it?"

He met the challenge in her voice and smiled, the expression lighting up his face. "Well, and who do you think it is? Your charming heart-throb, Tybalt?"

"I know who it is."

The smile dissolved, and Merky gripped her arm. "You know — how can you know? No one does."

"You're wrong there. Three people know. Me, Sarah, and you."

Arthur was giggling, and they turned stricken faces toward him, wondering what he found humorous. "I didn't call you, I didn't call you. That'll make Sarah hopping mad again. That's what I wanted."

"Call me where?" Merky snapped. "What is it, you imbecile?"

"He means he was supposed to call you and tell you to stay at the house instead of bringing the dog. They found me a long time ago," Julie told him apprehensively, yet glad he had spent that time searching through the snow for someone who wasn't even lost.

Merky cursed beneath his breath, kicking

out at Caesar, who was running in excited circles and yapping with pleasure at their impromptu game. "Shut up, you stupid dog." Caesar backed off and growled. "We'd better get back before Gerald wakes up," Merky decided, seizing Julie.

If she could get back to Avon House, the whole thing could blow up in their faces, for the police would arrive and she would be able to tell them everything. Unwittingly Sarah had outsmarted herself this time. This thought gave Julie comfort. She stepped out smartly, keeping pace with the men, though it left her breathless. Her head still hurt, and now her arm, which had suffered Sarah's hammerlike grip, was aching as if it were broken.

The old house emerged through the trees, casting its strange, forbidding shadow across the snow-covered lawns. Battlements zigzagged in grotesque parody in the moonlight. There were no cars parked before the entrance, and Julie's heart sank to her soaking feet.

"Well, looks like we're in time," Merky observed, glancing toward the twisting drive for the glimmer of headlights. "We'll go in by the garden room. It's unlocked. Tie this round her mouth." Merky handed Arthur a silk scarf, and Arthur obliged, tying the knot carefully.

Stumbling over garden baskets and the

spindly legs of potted-fern holders, they emerged none the worse into the dark, silent corridor. Sniffing the air, Caesar took off, disappearing in a black flash around the staircase.

"Where's that brute going?" Merky growled, but knowing he could never catch the dog, he dismissed the idea of pursuit. "Never mind. We won't need him."

Arthur was looking about in awe, and he reached for the light switch so that he could better admire the furnishings.

"Don't do that," Merky hissed, grabbing his arm. "Do you want to advertise our presence?"

As they entered the living room, where the glowing embers of a dying fire reddened the grate, the crunch of gravel betrayed the arrival of a car.

"Aha, no time for a drink, more's the pity. You, Arthur, take her out of here. There's a big cupboard we passed near the garden room — it's got plant pots and things in it. Push her in there. Hurry up. I'll hold them off at the door."

Obeying like an automaton, Arthur took Julie to the cupboard. Inside it cold air wafted from a vent in the wall. The glow of moonlight on the snow lit the tiny room with a strange light. With a flash of kindness he unfastened her gag.

"Don't go back there, Arthur. They're going to turn you in to the police," Julie urged, playing for time. Yet behind her warning there was a genuine concern for his welfare.

"I didn't do anything. No need to hide." He looked at the stacked terracotta pots and blue patterned bowls. "This is a pretty. I'd like to live here."

With a sigh of exasperation Julie resigned herself to whatever fate held in store. Arthur, with his curious obsession for beauty, was lost to her. He was fingering the raised design on a large tub with brass legs when sounds from the front of the house caught his attention, and he stepped out of the cupboard.

"Be sure to tell them you didn't do anything," Julie cautioned, but, intent on fastening the padlock on the door, he did not hear her.

Thumping steps told her he was going away, and she shivered, straining her ears for some sounds of life. Nothing but plant pots, not even any tools with which to batter at the door. At least he had loosened her gag, but shouting inside this cupboard with its thick door was next to useless. Where was everybody? Gerald must be in his own suite of rooms somewhere in the musty depths of the upper story. There was no one around; even the students who helped with the banquet had not put in an appearance since Friday. No one was likely to saunter by this door, for the garden room seemed to be Sarah's special interest — and Caesar's. He often lolled out here in the shelter of the potted ferns, awaiting a companion for walks. If only he would come to sniff the door and set up his fantastic chorus of barks, that would bring someone in a hurry.

Julie's eyes roamed the neat stacks of plant pots, and a brilliant idea made her smile with near-delight. Plant pots broke; they made loud noises. She could last for thirty minutes in here with so many to break, and by that time surely someone would be aroused.

She started with the blue one with its raised design, smashing it with an ear-shattering crash; then she used the brass legs to pound on the door. No one came. The lowest shelf went next, and she crashed the pottery against each other for maximum effect. The heap on the floor was growing when she heard a bumping snuffle from the other side of the door during one of her trial pauses.

"Caesar, good boy. Get your master — go on, get him," Julie hissed, crouching near the bottom of the door. Caesar yipped twice in recognition. Gerald might be fatally ill, he might be a Shakespearean maniac, but according to Sarah, he was quite innocent of this evening's frightening events. He was Julie's only hope.

The dog did not return. She broke some more pots, pushing them aside to make room. In the next pause she heard a scrabbling on the door, and thinking it was Caesar, she called his name. Instead of a woof, her answer was the clinking of the lock. The door opened, and she fell into someone's arms.

"Please help me," she cried to the dark, towering figure, knowing it was not Sarah and that it was too tall for Merky.

"Now, now, my dear. Don't get hysterical. You're safe with me. I might seem a bit of a fool, but I assure you, contrary to popular opinion, I have most of my faculties."

Gerald took her weight against his arm, his fraility of Friday evening not apparent. Julie blinked in surprise; in the gray-tinged light his face seemed to glow with a health and vigor belying his age. "But you're not ill, are you?" she gasped in surprise.

Gerald chuckled. "On the contrary, rather bursting with vulgar good health. Delighted I took you in on that little scene. I thought it was very touching."

"But why?"

"I had my reasons. A few greedy relatives squabbling for the spoils like carrion crows. Need I say more?"

183

Julie shook her head. So Gerald had suspected Sarah and Merky all along, and the story of his limited time on earth had been another of his death scenes; only this one was set in modern dress. Perhaps he knew more about Sarah's plans than she suspected. "You're something else," she managed with a rueful smile, struggling against his embrace.

"Why, thank you. Coming from such a charming girl, that's a real compliment." He beamed, his hooded eyes kindling a gleam of pleasure. "What I'd like to know is — what's going on? Why, my dear, are you destroying my valuable pottery inside a locked cupboard?"

"It's a long story. Come on, the police are in the living room."

Gerald caught his breath in surprise. "By Jove! Police! I thought they must be friends of my son's. By all means, my dear, let's see what little fiasco he has arranged."

When they entered the living room, the group of people seated before the sputtering fire stared at them with mingled reactions. On Sarah's face were fury and disbelief; Merky registered surprise and unease; the policeman, frank curiosity.

"Hello, I'm Gerald Brookham. Can I help you?" Gerald surged forward to the policeman, overwhelming him with his forceful presence.

"Sorry to trouble you, Mr. Brookham, at such a late hour." The man in the dark suit stood, his hand outstretched. "Lon Rogers, Winton Police Department." He offered his identification as Gerald looked askance at his lack of uniform. "I was at a family party, sir," the policeman offered in explanation. We haven't much in the way of a department over there."

"Gerald, dear, in view of your health, don't you think it would be better to leave all this unpleasantness to Mercutio?" Sarah cooed, coming to him and taking his elbow solicitously as she led him to a chair.

To her amazement Julie watched him crumple before her eyes, growing old and feeble as he shuffled slowly to the fireside, stretching near-transparent hands to the blaze.

"Yes, by all means, carry on."

Unable to stand the charade any longer, Julie cried, "Stop it, all of you! That girl at the police station told the truth. Everything Sandi says has happened. They're even going to pin the campus attacks on Arthur, and he's never even been to Smith!"

All eyes were riveted on her, and the policeman cleared his throat. "Well, that's certainly interesting, ma'am. No one's told me who you are."

"Julie Brown, the victim of the evening."

The policeman smiled. "Now I know. That little girl sure was steamed up about imprisonments and murders. I think she'd been having a bit too much to drink. Without Mrs. Brookham's help we might have had to launch more of an investigation. Anyway, put yourself in her hands. Sleep it off. You kids these days think you're indestructible." He stood, picking up his hat.

"What! Is this all you're going to do? When you're gone she'll murder me. She has to — I know too much about her. And about Merky. Poor Arthur's innocent."

"Julie, my dear, no one's accused Arthur of anything," Sarah soothed, moving toward her, her black eyes unfathomable. "As a matter of fact, the officer has a report fully made out with my cooperation. This is not *all* that's going to happen, as you put it. I'm afraid the real culprit will have to go quietly. I didn't want to do this, Merky; you know I've shielded you all this time."

A gasp echoed around the room, and Merky stared aghast at her, his face putty-colored with shock. "Me!"

"Yes. It's not easy to condemn one's own husband, but as poor Julie says, we can't allow anyone to think it's Arthur. My brother, though retarded, is quite harmless. These years have been a burden, but thankfully it'll

186

soon be over. I'm so sorry, Gerald; I had to do it." Crocodile tears edged down Sarah's strong-bridged nose as she patted Gerald's snowy head. He slumped dumbfounded before the fire. Merky tottered backward, bumping against a table loaded with ornaments.

"You liar! It's me who's shielded you!" he cried.

Sarah's eyes flashed. "How dare you?" She turned toward the policeman. "Of course, Officer, you know how impossible that accusation is. The assailant was a man."

"He did it. I saw him in town on Thursday night," Arthur announced startlingly as he appeared in the doorway.

Merky rounded on him in anger. "Shut up, you imbecile! Do you want me put away for the rest of my life! Be quiet!"

"There's this girl who works in the dough-nut shop. Every time he's here he goes to see her. I know."

"What's he talking about? What girl?" the policeman asked in astonishment, staring at Arthur, who bounded into the room, bubbling with his new discovery like an eager child.

Two figures followed him: Tybalt and a strange girl.

"Linda!" the policeman voiced in surprise. "Now, what are you doing here? I thought

Doc told you to get some rest," he chided the young blonde woman wearing a hooded purple, pile-edged coat.

"It's all right, Lon. Tybalt said I could help save someone's life. That's why I'm here." Glancing at Merky, she said, "He's the one. I'm sure because I've dated him."

Merky wobbled to a nearby chair. "Oh, God, none of you knows what I've had to put up with," he groaned, his head in his hands. "All right. I'll confess. I did grab Linda, but only because I wanted her to listen to me. She was going to break things off. I couldn't stand that. But she wouldn't listen — she wouldn't stop."

"You mean you knew who attacked you all along?" the policeman snapped at Linda, who sniffled in self-pity.

"Yes. But he was married. I felt kinda sorry for him. I guess that's why I didn't tell. But now you've got this other little guy." She smiled wanly at Arthur. "I just knew I had to turn him in."

"Two blueberry doughnuts and a cup of coffee, please," Arthur chanted with a grin. "Two blueberry doughnuts —"

"Shut up, Arthur. We don't want to know," Sarah said.

"There's someone else out in the hall. She came over from Winton in the police cruiser,"

Tybalt announced, turning as Sandi came into the room on the arm of a uniformed policeman.

"Thank the Lord you're okay, Julie," Sandi said. "Wow, did I have visions of you freezing in that darned cave! Tybalt came to your rescue, you ought to know that."

Julie gaped at her. "Tybalt? How did he do that?"

"I ran into him in Winton — literally. Last month I told him I'd seen the campus attacker once, but until an hour ago he didn't know exactly how. When I described his clothing, like a flash Tybalt came to some weird conclusions. Merky may have been operating in Winton last Saturday night, but the person who grabbed me was heavyset, with long dark hair, and smelled of after-shave lotion. I always figured it was some clean hippie, until we got to talking. This is what he wore." Sandi thrust a man's overcoat forward. A black, military-style coat with dull silver buttons. The coat Sarah had worn this evening during the hunt in the snow.

"Sarah!" At Julie's gasp Sarah became the focus of attention. Her usually smooth face lost some of its composure.

"What utter nonsense," she said flatly.

"Not really, Sarah. You weren't careful enough. All I had to do was look in your closet. During the struggle Sandi pulled a button from your cuff. You hadn't noticed, had you?" Tybalt held out a metal button with a military emblem on it. The policeman put it against the coat cuff where a thread dangled emptily.

"Well, I'll be darned. They match."

"It's a lie. That's circumstantial evidence. Anyone could have worn that coat. Even you, Tybalt," Sarah hissed.

Clearly wavering, the policeman reluctantly agreed. "She's right, you know. Unless you've something else to go on."

"We have. Sarah's been running a little campus drug operation ever since she came here. A former friend of ours, Deanie Jones, bought from her, but Sarah didn't know Deanie was going to blow the whistle about her to a girl friend. Up till now Sarah hasn't been sure which girl friend it was. That's why they were all attacked —"

"No, you're so wrong, Tybalt," Sarah interrupted, her voice dark with emotion. "So wrong. Did you really think that was the reason they were attacked? Did you think I would risk so much for something like that? You, my dear, were the reason. Every time I saw you with one of those simpering little idiots, with their long hair and empty faces, part of me died. You never really knew, did you, even when you lived here? Your mother, with her selfish, demanding ways, was like a saint to you."

Tybalt opened his mouth to protest, but decided against it when the others motioned him to be quiet. Sarah was lost to them all, pouring out her frustrations from her own tormented world.

"I saw how you loved Juliet Brookham. Watched how you let her touch you, until I hated her. What a waste she was. Such a useless piece of flesh. Not alive like me. I had to stop it. You never really noticed me. Don't you see — Merky was my only hope. Then I could stay near you. This house, you, Arthur; those were the only things I really wanted. We could have been happy. I wouldn't let Merky ruin things for me. He's expendable. If only you'd been kind. I loved you, Tybalt. I killed for you."

The silence that followed her words was profound, and though Julie had just cause to hate her, she found tears of pity choking in her throat for Sarah's misery.

"Come on, Mrs. Brookham. You can make a statement in town. You, too, Mr. Brookham."

Surprisingly Merky, looking as though he had been through a disaster, took Sarah's arm and guided his sobbing wife toward the door.

"Sorry for this, Father. Too bad you have to take these memories with you," he muttered in a tear-choked voice as he passed his father's chair.

The aged appearance dropped from Gerald as he rose with a smile. "I'm going nowhere, Mercutio, disappointing though that might be. Just a little trick of mine to test your mettle. Didn't fail, either."

Merky looked away. His face was drawn into a set expression of resignation as he shuffled into the hallway.

Hardly able to comprehend what had happened, Julie shook her head and began attempting to salvage her appearance, knowing what a total fright she must look in the bedraggled stage costume beneath Sarah's coat.

"Sorry if you thought I didn't believe you," Tybalt apologized throatily, his hand light against her cheek. "At first, I must admit, it was hard to take. When I finally accepted that you weren't some strung-out neurotic, things made more sense. Finding out I was so blind to Sarah's plans makes me ashamed. On an intelligence quotient I guess I rate about fifteen."

Julie smiled up at him in relief and pleasure, finding his grin infectious, the warmth of his open affection exhilarating. "Glad that you listened to me, anyway."

"Oh, I listened. Believing was something else. I always listen to girls, whatever wild things they say."

His arm was supportive as he took her to the fire. Now Julie realized she was numb, but whether from the cold or from emotional shock, she was not sure.

"Tybalt's going to be my heir. I'm so glad. Having to choose has been rather a bore," Gerald revealed, his eyes bright with humor. "About time I could get back to the real meat of life. Call that dreadful woman if you want some food. Do her good to have to wake up and cook. What do I pay her for, after all?" With that he sailed from the room, his voice rising in a quotation from *Hamlet*.

"Though probably neither of us is up to it tonight, how do you feel romantically?" Tybalt asked, his hand warm on her arm. "Guess we've both had enough time to think things over, decide how we really feel about each other. I'm tired of waiting for you to give me the word."

Julie looked around to see if they were alone. She felt embarrassed by the intimate implications of his words. Both Sandi and Arthur had left in the wake of the policemen. "How about a rain check?" she murmured, allowing her body to relax against the warmth of him, absorbing an exciting feeling of masculine protection.

"Hey, I don't see any rain," he laughed, his mouth inches from hers. They kissed, and this time she did not fight him off, allowing herself to succumb to the pleasure of his kiss.

"No, but you never can tell."

"I already know you don't think much of Avon House as a permanent residence, so where do you fancy? I think one of those job leaflets mentioned Guatemala."

"There was another I had my mind set on. How about the one in Paris?"

"That was for a couple, as I recall."

"Yes, I believe it was."

Tybalt stared at her uncomprehendingly a moment, then he began to laugh. "Say, Julie Brown, was that a proposal? Talk about women's lib!"

Julie smiled and nodded. His grip had not slackened on her hand, nor had he moved away. She was bold, assured, something she had not wholly been at any time before in her life. He gave her that needed anchor, the knowledge that she was important to someone. Now she did not mind Pete Jordan so much. If Mom was happy with him, wasn't that really all that mattered? Now that she had Tybalt, she could afford to let go.

"You've always been pretty good about

making proposals. Now it's my turn for a change," she said.

Tybalt pulled her closer, his hair tickling her brow, his eyes gleaming in the firelight. "You're right. And somehow yours seems much more appealing."

We hope you have enjoyed this Large Print book. Other Thorndike Press or Chivers Press Large Print books are available at your library or directly from the publishers.

For more information about current and upcoming titles, please call or write, without obligation, to:

Thorndike Press
P.O. Box 159
Thorndike, Maine 04986 USA
Tel. (800) 257-5157

OR

Chivers Press Limited
Windsor Bridge Road
Bath BA2 3AX
England
Tel. (0225) 335336

All our Large Print titles are designed for easy reading, and all our books are made to last.